Summer Stock

VANESSA NORTH

D1622535

RIPTIDE
PUBLISHING

Riptide Publishing
PO Box 1537
Burnsville, NC 28714
www.riptidepublishing.com

Summer Stock

Cover art: L.C. Chase, lcchase.com/design.htm
Editor: Carole-ann Galloway
Layout: L.C. Chase, lcchase.com/design.htm

ISBN: 978-1-62649-569-2

First edition
May, 2017

Also available in ebook:
ISBN: 978-1-62649-568-5

Summer Stock

VANESSA
NORTH

RIPTIDE
PUBLISHING

To my buddy Hank, and to everyone else who would rather smell flowers than fight.

Table of
Contents

Chapter One

Ryan woke in a strange bed with a splitting headache and a stale mouth.

Shit. What happened? He had a vague memory of a brawny townie smiling at him over a margarita laced with jalapeño peppers, and then later—*how many drinks later?*—spicy-hot kisses and a low chuckle and a pool of want in his gut. A promising beginning—too bad he couldn't remember what had come next. He rolled onto his back and flinched as his muscles protested the movement.

A glance to his left granted him a peek at his hookup from the night before. Soft golden stubble on a square jaw. A cauliflower ear. Ryan blinked—had he gone to bed with a boxer? Then his eyes traced the high, chiseled cheekbones, ruddy from sunshine. They flanked a nose that could charitably be called *distinctive*, and soft, full lips twitched around a snore.

For about half a second, Ryan looked at those lips, remembered jalapeños, and thought about waking the guy up for another round—one he'd be sober enough to remember. Then it hit him like a freight train.

He was in *North Carolina*. Not to shoot a TV show or a movie or anything real. No, his ass had been banished to this backwater in disgrace. To do *summer stock*.

So what if he'd gone willingly? If he'd asked—begged—his cousin Caro to get him a job like they were teenagers again and he was too shy to ask the manager of the Piggly Wiggly if they needed weekend baggers?

He wouldn't have had to ask if there hadn't been an ultimatum.

"Stay out of the tabloids or find another agent. You're on your third publicist in a year. I can't get you work if I'm constantly bailing you out of trouble with the press."

Ryan glanced down at the snoring townie. Having drunk hookups with strangers—of any sex, but particularly male strangers—might be exactly the sort of thing Mike would consider *trouble*. What exactly had they done the night before? Had there been drugs? The room didn't have the stale smell he associated with regular pot smoking. He looked around. No bongs. Better still, no mirrors lying out on the horizontal surfaces. It appeared the damage from their party was confined to margaritas and that lamp they'd knocked over on the way to the bed.

But where were his clothes?

Gingerly, he eased himself out of the bed and peeked underneath it. A single white sock—not his—and a pair of filthy Converse, again *not his*. The dark-stained hardwood floor was clean except for the lamp, and his clothes were nowhere to be seen. He racked his brain for a memory, any memory, of their arrival at the townie's apartment. Did the guy have roommates? If Ryan opened the door and walked into the living room, would someone see his wedding tackle hanging out?

He tried the door anyway, freezing when a muffled groan emerged from the blankets. But the townie just pulled a pillow over his head and rolled onto his stomach. Poor bastard was probably as hungover as Ryan.

Oh so slowly, Ryan eased the door open, wincing as it creaked. He was in luck. His shirt was on the floor outside the bedroom door, and when he picked it up, he discovered one of his socks, a little smelly, but no worse for wear. He pulled on the T-shirt and kept moving. He came around the corner into a bright living room dominated by a massive sectional. His attention was immediately drawn to a flat-screen that would be the envy of any home theater aficionado, but then he spied the other sock beside the couch.

No sign of roommates or family members. So far, so good. When he spotted his jeans thrown over the back of the sectional, he grabbed them, then froze again as a memory washed over him.

"Keep your hands on the back of the sofa," in a rumbling coastal drawl.

The pants fell to the floor as he remembered the stranger's rough hands on his body and a stubbled kiss along his spine. The recall evoked a flash of mind-bending pleasure, and he nearly moaned out loud. Clearly, they'd had a good time. But where the hell was his underwear? He dropped to his knees and peeked under the sofa. Nothing.

A quick stroll around the couch didn't reveal their whereabouts either.

He was just about to give up and go commando, when a low snarl ripped through the air. Turning slowly, he cupped one hand protectively over his junk.

In a corner of the room, on what appeared to be a twin-sized mattress, the biggest dog he'd ever seen was growling at him.

It had to weigh two hundred pounds. Pendulous jowls shook as the dog emitted another threat. There, clutched between the dog's gigantic paws, was Ryan's favorite pair of briefs. As he watched with growing horror, the hellhound leaned over, snuffled his prize, and started chewing on them.

Speechless, horrified, and naked from the waist down, Ryan did the only thing that occurred to him.

He ran.

Sheer terror swamped him as he shoved open the front door. Was the dog going to decide to come straight for the source of his new favorite snack? Ryan didn't care if roommates, neighbors, or the baby Jesus himself saw his wedding tackle. He was *not* about to stick around and get eaten by a dog. No matter how tempting those flashes of bend-me-over-the-couch-and-have-your-way-with-me sex were.

It wasn't until he was halfway down the driveway that he realized he'd left his pants on the floor, and his phone was still in the pocket.

And that was when the paparazzi showed up.

Trey pulled the pillow down over his ears. Ryan had scrambled out of bed without so much as a peck on the cheek and an *It's been nice.*

At first Trey had wondered if he'd gotten up to go to the bathroom, but then the front door had slammed with a sordid finality.

Rude.

And a little insulting. Trey didn't have much of an ego to bruise—he knew he wasn't a catch—but he thought they'd had *fun*. He wouldn't normally even try to hook up with a guy who looked like he could be in movies, but the way Ryan had stared at him last night had gone straight to his head. Both heads. And from what he'd been able to tell, Ryan had been into it—laughing and flirting and kissing like he'd die if they didn't. God, those kisses. Trey hadn't kissed like that in years. With Ryan's hands in Trey's hair and whimpers in his throat and his chest heaving like he'd just dashed the two hundred meter. A spike of pleasure at the memory had soured into resentment when Ryan snuck out of the house. Hell, maybe beautiful people didn't go in for morning cuddling and pancakes, but they could at least say good-bye, right?

Trey flopped over onto his back and winced at the frisson of pain slithering from his skull down his spine. He'd had too much to drink, and he'd pay for it the rest of the day.

One of Ferdinand's thunderous barks ripped through the house. Someone was knocking—at seven o'clock on a Sunday morning? Throwing his pillow to the side, he sprang up out of bed before the dog really got going and tore up the coffee table again. He grabbed a pair of boxers out of the basket of clean laundry and pulled them on.

Ryan was at the front door.

Without his pants.

Had he taken a wrong turn on the way to the bathroom and ended up outside? Trey's heart leaped. Ryan hadn't been sneaking out without saying good-bye after all. They could still have pancakes and some cuddling. He wanted to explore that cute constellation of freckles on Ryan's shoulders more closely, and hear him laugh, and maybe kiss him until they forgot their hangovers.

Trey started to open the door, but Ryan shouted, "Whoa!" and held up his hands in the universal signal for stop.

It was like cold water thrown in Trey's face.

So, no pancakes then.

"What do you want?" Trey asked.

Ryan looked over his shoulder, then back at Trey.

"Can you hand me my pants? And my Birks?"

"Were you in so much of a hurry to get away that you forgot your pants?"

Ryan actually smiled. "Yes! Exactly. Do you mind just passing them through the crack in the door? You can keep the underwear."

You have got to be kidding me.

"Did you hit your head on something while I was sleeping?" Trey gritted his teeth and glared as his headache roared back to life.

"Not that I know of." Ryan glanced around, clearly agitated. "My pants? Please? There's a kid out here taking pictures."

Trey scanned the room. The sandals were by the door; he picked those up and thrust them through the crack at Ryan. When he crossed to the couch to collect Ryan's fancy designer jeans, the door closed with a bang behind him.

That's it. He grabbed the jeans, stalked to the front door, flung it *all the way open*, and tossed them right in Ryan's face.

"Have a nice life, asshole."

He slammed the door shut and locked it. Behind him, Ferdinand barked once, then whined.

Trey turned around and looked at the dog, who was sitting with his head tilted to the side and long strings of drool hanging from his mouth.

"Yeah, I don't get it either, Peanut. Let's make pancakes."

He should have known Ferdinand would be a better breakfast companion than some pretty boy anyway.

Mason dropped the newspaper on his desk and glared at Ryan. In Mason's office, a tiny room behind the box office, mosquitoes congregated on the one grimy window, lending the place a sinister vibe, but aside from the front page section of the *Banker's Shoals Herald*, Mason's desk was clear.

As was his point.

"Do you think this press is what Shakespeare by the Sea needs?"

Ryan flinched at the steely cold in Mason's voice. He'd known Mason since they were kids—Mason had been best friends forever with Ryan's cousin Caroline. Ryan had idolized Mason for years, and was embarrassed to be called into the office for a dressing down. He couldn't meet Mason's gaze, so he looked at the newspaper, where his own pasty-white ass cheeks were plastered across the front page. Below the fold, of course. This was a *family-oriented* town. But there they were. And they did *not* give credit to the million hours a week Ryan spent at the gym. As for that headline . . .

Hollywood Playboy Bryan Hart Caught Streaking in Banker's Shoals!

"I'm sorry."

"You are here because Caro said please. You are here because Caro *promised* me you would stay out of trouble. You are here because my goddamn theater is bleeding money and you agreed to work for free. Do not hammer the nail in my coffin, boy, unless you plan to share it."

The unfairness of it all soured in Ryan's stomach. Shame boiled under the surface, the kind of shame that would usually make him lash out, but Mason was right. He was here because Caro had offered him a safe place to land when he'd fallen, and he wasn't going to repay her by putting her theater out of business. So, humiliating as it was, he sucked it up and told the truth.

Well. Sort of.

"I wasn't streaking. I met someone," he began. "I know you don't understand, because you're a monk."

"I am not a monk." Mason's nostrils flared.

"Asexual, then. Whatever." Ryan waved it away.

"Don't use words you don't understand. Keep talking."

"I met someone. And yes, I slept with them on the first date; we do that in Hollywood sometimes."

One of Mason's eyebrows quirked up at the pronoun, but he didn't say anything.

Ryan didn't want to inadvertently out anyone, so gender-neutral pronouns were best. He brightened a little—maybe Trey was in the closet and this would never go beyond the two of them. Ryan's face burned hotter. It was hardly fair to hope his hookup was closeted just because his own bisexuality was inconvenient.

"I was really into them, and somehow on our way to bed, I missed the fact that they have this enormous man-eating dog."

"Man-eating, huh?"

Was that a bit of a smile lingering around Mason's lips? Mason was a good-looking dude: a big black man with gleaming white teeth, a shaved head, and a propensity for wearing tight T-shirts. Ryan liked Mason's smile—had always liked Mason's smile—so he played to his audience.

"Mason, man, I'm telling you, this beast was four hundred pounds and already snacking on my Andrew Christians. I was running for my life."

Mason did smile then, and Ryan felt a twitch of relief. Short-lived, because Mason pointed down at the picture, the one where Ryan was banging on the front door of Trey's duplex with his ass exposed.

"I admit, here in the theater, we don't know much about cinematography, but this doesn't appear to be an action shot, Ry."

Nicknames. Nicknames were good. Snide comments about theater versus film were bad. Jesus, talking to a pissed-off Mason was like walking a tight rope.

"I forgot my phone," Ryan mumbled.

"I see. So let me get this straight: you were running for your life from a four-hundred-pound, man-eating beast who was flossing with your Andrew Christians, and you returned straight into the jaws of certain death in order to retrieve your phone?"

"Well, the nearest Apple store is in Raleigh and that's *hours* away."

"Remind me why I cast you again?"

"Because I'm working pro bono?"

Mason's smile fell. "I told you not to use words you don't understand. Your cousin—who is worth a dozen of you—thinks the sun rises and sets out of this—" Mason's finger landed on the paper, right on Ryan's butt "—lily-white ass. So grow up. Get your shit together, Ry. I don't want to see your stage name in the *Herald* unless it's in the context of a 'who knew he could actually act?' review. Got it?"

"Yes, sir."

"Good. Now get out of my sight. Call is at seven Monday morning for the read through."

"I'll be there."

"In pants, please."

Ryan flushed. He was never going to live this down. Nodding, he started for the door.

"One more thing," Mason said.

"Yeah?" Ryan looked over his shoulder. Mason didn't meet his eyes, instead he was scribbling something in a notebook.

"The cast and crew are off-limits. You want to screw around, do it elsewhere. I don't need drama in my theater."

"No problem. I don't date people in the business."

"As long as we're clear on that."

"Crystal."

Chapter Two

Trey sat in the tiny waiting room, staring at the Bible verse on the wall, with the smell of lavender heavy in his nostrils. He didn't find Bible verses or lavender comforting, but Dr. Wharton's new-age music wasn't so bad. It suited the soothing blue walls and the seashell paintings. Across the room, a sullen teenager glared at him and shoved earbuds into her ears.

He looked down at his knee, which was bouncing with the nervous energy he couldn't quite hold back whenever he sat here.

The door in the corner opened, its familiar creak drawing Trey's gaze. The doctor smiled at him, all big hair and kind eyes. "Come on, Trey." She turned to the teenager. "Ava?" The girl tugged one of her earbuds out and glanced up. "Katelyn's going to do your med check today, okay?" The girl nodded, shoved the earbud back into place, and returned her attention to her phone.

Trey followed Dr. Wharton down the hall to her office, where she gestured at the chair and sat behind her desk. He perched on the edge of the seat, not ready to sink into it and let go of the gnawing irritation of pride.

"How was your week? How's Ferdinand?"

She was fighting dirty today. He straightened his spine and studied his fingernails. "He's fine. The lump was a benign cyst."

"Good. I know that was weighing heavily on you last week. How is work?"

He glanced up at her then, and she smiled, dimples carving grooves into her tanned cheeks. Slumping back in the chair, he sighed. "It's fine. The actors are coming in for the read through on Monday morning, then my crew is going to start the sets for *Julius Caesar*."

"So, Ferdy's fine. Work's fine. And how are you, Trey? Are you fine too?"

Resentment pushed at him, and he couldn't quite put his finger on why. "I hooked up with someone a couple nights ago. A tourist, I guess. I met him at that tacky place on the beach with the jalapeño margaritas."

"That tacky place that your sister owns?" The laughter in her voice tugged his lips up in answer.

"Yeah, that one." He loved his sister, loved that she and her husband had opened one of their restaurants here on Banker's Shoals so they could be close to him—but the reason why rankled.

"Are you going to see him again?"

Jesus, what part of *hookup* didn't she understand? "No. I didn't even get his number. It was a hookup," he repeated, as if that explained the sudden flare of anger that had him tightening his grip on the chair's arm.

"What drew you to him?"

His laugh. His face. He stared at my lips like he was hungry. Being wanted is such a turn-on. Trey shrugged. "I don't know."

"So, why did you bring him up?"

He glared at her. "You're my shrink, you tell me."

She folded her hands on her desk in the way that meant she wasn't falling for his shit, the way that meant he was going to fucking cry, *again*.

"He was laughing. You know, like—" Trey threw his head back and laughed in a gruesome imitation of Ryan's carefree cackle. "Like he didn't care what he looked like or who was watching. Like he was having the time of his life. It was fun."

"Well, good. I'm glad you had fun. How's your sister?"

"Overworked. Bossy. Pregnant." He smiled, relieved at the change of subject, because Kim's pregnancy announcement was the best news he'd had all year. He'd been high-spirited, giddy even, for the first time in months. It was no wonder Ryan's laugh had drawn him in that night—a good mood, shared, seemed to multiply.

Her eyebrow shot up. "Congratulations. That's exciting."

"Yeah. I'm gonna be an uncle for the sixth time."

"And you feel good about that?"

"Of course. I love kids. Ferdy loves kids too, so." He relaxed back into the chair a little more. "I'm really happy for Kim and Danny."

"Please give them my congratulations."

He nodded.

"So, have you made any progress on the garage?"

He'd known the question was coming, had felt it hovering over him like the blade of a guillotine, but hearing the words out loud in the office still tightened his chest until he couldn't—

"Breathe," she reminded him.

He choked in a gasp, then exhaled it as he shook his head. "I can't. I started clearing off his toolbox, and I got all panicky. I took a Xanax, and I started to feel better, but then I got sleepy. I can't do it if I'm not awake for it, and I can't do it without the Xanax. It's too much."

"Okay. That's okay. What did you do after you took the Xanax and got sleepy?"

"I locked the door and watched TV with Ferdy."

"Good. Are you going to try again this week?"

"I don't know." He shook his head, panic and shame tangling in his gut. "I don't want to."

"I know you don't want to. But think how good it will feel to reclaim that space for yourself. He's not coming back, and it's okay to use that space."

"I know. I'm just . . . I see his things. I see them, and it's so awful, Doc. I don't know how to do it."

"One step at a time. Three months ago you couldn't open the door. You're doing fine. Maybe next time, try taking Ferdinand with you. See if his presence helps you feel safe, okay?"

"Yeah." That was a good idea. He could try that. Ferdy was almost as good as Xanax.

"Trey."

He looked up at her again. "Yeah?"

"You're doing fine. You know that, right? You're doing fine."

"Okay." He didn't feel fine. He felt like a mess. A mess who couldn't even walk into his own garage without having a panic attack.

"Recovering from your physical injuries was easy compared to the work you're doing now. You're a strong man, Trey. You've accomplished a lot. But it's hard work."

"I know." He did. Therapy left him wrung out and exhausted and most weeks he left with his eyes swollen from all the tears he couldn't seem to stop. Angry tears, ashamed tears. He could feel them now, pricking at his eyes and stinging his nose.

"What happened to you wasn't your fault. Vincent is the only one to blame."

The name hit him like a punch to the face.

"He—" No matter how hard he swallowed, he couldn't speak around the lump in his throat.

"He's not coming back, Trey. He's in jail, and he's never going to hurt you again."

"I brought tequil— Wow." Caro took two steps into the house and froze, jaw hanging open. "This is the nicest rental house I've ever seen. Holy shit, how much are you paying for this place?"

Ryan flinched. "Um, it's not a rental."

"You bought it? You bought a *house*? Are you fucking kidding me? You told me you would never move back to the island. You told me—"

"I didn't buy it; it's West Brady's place."

She closed the door behind her and spun in a circle, clearly taking in the magazine-ready decor. "Has anyone ever told him his name is backward?"

A swell of affection rose in Ryan's chest. Of course Caro would go there—irreverent, unfazeable Caro. As much a part of Banker's Shoals as the sand and the salt and the sea air. Caro had no fucks for West Hollywood *or* West Brady. If he weren't her cousin, would she have any fucks to give for Bryan Hart?

"I honestly don't think anyone would dare."

"How do you know West Brady? Doesn't he direct all those teenage romantic comedies? The next John Hughes or something like that?"

"Yeah. We met at a party a few years ago; we're friends-ish."

Raising an eyebrow, Caro crossed her arms over her chest. "Ish?"

"He dated Ali for a few years—she introduced us." It was still weird for Ryan to think of West and Ali's relationship in the past tense—their recent breakup had stunned him. "He practically lived in our house when he wasn't on location."

"West Brady dated your girlfriend. And he owns a house on Banker's Shoals by coincidence?"

"She's not my girlfriend; she's my roommate. And no, he owns a house on Banker's Shoals because I talked about it so much he vacationed here last year and decided to buy a place. Look, he's a good guy. He let me borrow his house for the summer." *And if I get my shit together, he might have a role for me when I go back to LA.*

"Okay. I'm sorry. One of these days you'll have to explain the whole Ali thing, but I'm not going to grill you about it tonight. Margaritas?" She held up the bottle of tequila, and Ryan flinched, remembering jalapeños and a hangover.

"Why don't I open a bottle of wine instead?"

"Ryan Hertzog drinking wine? What is the world coming to? Do you even know the difference between a Chardonnay and a Chablis?"

"I learned from Bryan Hart." Ryan took the bottle of tequila from Caro's hands. "Get comfy and pick a movie. Prosecco okay?"

"Sounds fab." She kicked off her shoes and dropped onto the couch with a contented sigh, reaching for the remote.

West Brady's kitchen was a work of art. All gleaming metal and marble. Ryan set the tequila on the counter and made his way to the glass-fronted Sub-Zero wine fridge. He recognized the labels on many of the bottles from a trip to Napa with West and Ali. West had been madly in love with Ali, willing to do anything she wanted in bed, and when she'd said that she wanted to watch him and Ryan together, he'd laughed and gamely collected Ryan and brought him into their circle of gentle affection. They hadn't loved him the way they loved each other, but they'd made him feel good, and he'd done his best to give back in return. The three of them had spent idyllic nights sprawled together in a giant bed and their days soaking up sunshine and wine lore.

With a sudden pang, he missed Ali—his roommate, his confidante, and the best damned friend he had. He pulled his phone out of his pocket and shot her a quick text.

I miss you, baby.

She wouldn't get the text right away. She wasn't allowed to have her cell phone in rehab. He had no idea when she'd get the message, but the thought of her face, and how she'd smile when she finally saw it—and she would, she'd smile that special smile that was only for him—it made him smile too. He grabbed two glasses and a bottle of the prosecco he loved—something below Bryan Hart's or West Brady's pay grade, but perfect for shy Ryan Hertzog from Banker's Shoals, North Carolina—and made his way back to the living room.

Caro was sitting on the couch with her long legs crossed under her and her hair tumbling in wild curls around her shoulders. "*Beach House* is on Netflix."

"Oh no. No, no, no, no." The "reality" show he'd done four years ago, the one where he and Ali had been paired as the celebrity—him—and the average Jane—ha, like there was anything average about Ali—competing against nine other pairs was an embarrassment to his career and hers. It had given him the best friend of his heart, but it wasn't exactly a bright spot on his résumé.

"Come on, it'll be so much fun."

"It's gross. I can't believe it's still available for streaming."

The familiar title music blared from West's surround sound, and Ryan shook his head, resigned to the humiliation because it was Caro, and yeah, he could sit through this for some quality time with his cousin.

"You guys were so cute." She hugged a pillow to her chest and cackled as he poured the wine. "Look how young you were!"

"Yeah, yeah." He handed over her glass.

"Thank you." She took it from him and smiled before raising it high. "To summer stock, and having you home."

"To summer stock and home," he echoed, clinking their glasses together. Joining her on the couch, he took a deep sip of the wine and let the bubbles wash over his tongue. She cuddled up to him and laid her head on his shoulder, and for the first time since his plane touched down in Raleigh, he really did feel like he was home.

Chapter Three

The start of summer stock season reminded Trey of the first day of school when he'd been a kid. Nervous anticipation fluttered through his body as he turned off his alarm and pulled on a pair of shorts. A 7 a.m. call meant his morning walk on the beach with Ferdy coincided with a stunning red and gold sunrise over the Atlantic. Trey kicked off his sneakers and let the cool surf wash over his feet, as he shivered with delight. The morning felt special, in no small part due to his eagerness to hear the season's plays for the first time. He'd worked for Shakespeare by the Sea every summer for the last five years, building sets and helping Caroline Hertzog with whatever she needed. Aside from a few regulars, the cast changed year by year, but the crew? They were family.

Nothing could dampen Trey's mood as he strode through the doors of the playhouse, not even being handed a nondisclosure agreement for some second-rate TV actor who was padding out his résumé doing live theater. Trey scribbled his signature at the bottom of the form, handed it back to Mason's assistant director, and went searching for Caro and Mason.

And then he heard that laugh.

The last time he'd heard it had been in his bedroom, sated and sleepy. How anyone could make a sound filled with that much joy was a wonder to him, and he couldn't help a rueful smile as he rounded the corner into Mason's office.

"Trey! Come meet my cousin, Ryan." Caro perched on Mason's desk, facing the door while Mason sat behind the desk like a king in his throne room, grinning at the man opposite him. *Ryan*.

Trey's breath caught in his throat when Ryan turned to greet him. He had thought maybe he'd embellished in hindsight, that his hookup couldn't have been that handsome, but there was no denying Ryan was the most beautiful person he'd seen in his life. And the way he was looking at Trey now, with surprise and warmth and a hint of shyness—it struck Trey down to his bones. How was it possible this was the same guy who'd scurried out of his house so fast he'd forgotten his pants?

"We've met, actually." Ryan stood up and shone the full wattage of his smile on Trey, holding out his hand. "It's nice to see you again."

Ryan's hand was warm and dry, softly callused, like he worked out in a gym without gloves, but not like Trey's own tool-roughened hands.

"Yeah, it's . . ." Ryan's playful hazel gaze stopped Trey in his tracks. Who was this guy? ". . . nice."

"I can't believe you know Trey Donovan, Ry!" Caro practically screeched, drawing Trey's attention away from her cousin. "Mase, did you know about this?"

Mason's eyes widened slightly, then he opened his hands and shrugged. "I had no idea, Caro." His voice seemed too pat, too unconcerned, and Trey glanced back at Ryan to see an embarrassed flush creeping up his face.

"We met at Kim's place," Trey volunteered—anything to cover the awkward moment between Ryan and his cousin. "You know she's got those new jalapeño margaritas."

Ryan smiled slyly. "And I had a few too many of them, so Trey made sure I didn't try to sleep on the beach like when I was in high school. But I don't remember you from high school. Did you go to BS High?"

Trey shook his head. "Nah. I moved here from Savannah with my . . ." swallowing hard, he muscled through the words ". . . with my ex-husband. I've been working for Caro and Mason for five summers. I mean, I do other stuff the rest of the year. Donovan Remodeling." He fished a card out of his pocket and handed it over, worried it might be covered with sweat, but who the fuck cared at this point? "Here for all your household needs."

"Good to know." Ryan tucked the card into his pocket. "Well, call is in fifteen and I haven't met the rest of the cast yet, so I'm gonna mosey out to the stage area. It really is nice to see you, Trey."

Trey would have been fine with that, would have considered himself dismissed, except that just as Ryan was walking out the door, he paused and glanced over his shoulder, lower lip caught between his teeth.

The movement would have seemed practiced on anyone else Trey knew, but on Ryan it appeared sweet and utterly guileless. Innocent.

And one thing Trey knew after their explosive night together? Ryan was far from innocent.

"I'd better go make sure he doesn't get in any trouble." Mason gave Caro a weak smile, then hurried out of the room after Ryan.

Folding her arms across her chest, Caro watched him go with an expression that hovered somewhere between exasperated and bemused, then she focused on Trey, and he was struck by the family resemblance. The upturned hazel eyes that looked fey and enchanting on Ryan were more careworn and lined on Caro, but just as playful. Her brown hair was streaked by sunshine and salt air, and Ryan's by peroxide and professionals, but the effect was the same. The genuine kindness in her smile was every bit as warm as Ryan's, and he wondered if they learned that kindness from each other. He'd gotten the feeling before that Caro had had a rough childhood—her knowledge of navigating the justice system for victims of domestic violence had been a godsend to him eighteen months ago, but since she'd never explained how she'd come by that knowledge, he'd never wanted to pry.

"Hey, you okay?" She prodded his knee. "I lost you for a minute there."

He smiled back at her. "Yeah. I was just thinking how much you resemble your cousin. I'm surprised I didn't see it when I met him."

A blush spread across her freckled cheeks, and she studied her hands. "Thanks, Trey. You're very sweet."

Well I'll be damned. Trey hadn't ever thought of Caro as the kind of woman who would be easily flattered—but he'd never imagined she'd blush at a simple observation either.

"You're a beautiful woman, you must know that, right?"

She swallowed and glanced at the door. "It's hard to believe other people think so. I'm a behind-the-scenes kind of girl. I always have been, and I always will be."

Rubbing her hands together, she jumped down from the desk. "Are you ready to go listen to the read through? I'd love to hear some of your set ideas for this year's plays, and we have a new lighting designer who studied at UNC-Asheville and knows theater in the round techniques. We can all sit in the back and pass notes."

"Yeah, that sounds good."

"You knew, didn't you? Who my hookup was when I told you that story about the dog?" Ryan cornered Mason outside the theater during a break in the read through. Mason lit a cigarette and grinned at him.

"Why else do you think I made you promise to stay away from the crew?"

"Bastard." Ryan reached for Mason's front pocket and snatched the pack. "Gimme your lighter."

"No." Mason grabbed the cigarettes back. "Caro would kill me if you start smoking again."

"So I can't get laid and I can't smoke?"

"You can get laid all you want. But stay the fuck away from Trey Donovan. He's too good for you."

That felt like a punch to the solar plexus. "Wow, that's a shitty thing to say to an old friend."

"You have no idea how many shitty things I want to say to you." Mason's finger came out and poked him in the chest. "Your cousin has been worried to death about you for *years*. Drugs, drinking, partying. God only knows what the hell else with that woman."

"Ali is my best friend," Ryan gritted out. "And she's a brilliant actress."

"She's in rehab, and you should be too."

"I'm not— God, it's not like that. I don't even really like all that shit. I just . . . I just went along with Ali. Sure, I'd do a bump here and there, but I'm not some cokehead. Hollywood is a hard place.

It's hard work." He ran a hand through his hair. It sounded like he was complaining about a life other people envied, people like Mason, who instead of directing movies, was directing summer stock in North Carolina. "It's harder for women, like it is for black guys."

Mason's head came up at that. "What do you know about—"

"Ali needs to let go sometimes, but she never knows when to stop. I was there to protect her. That's what friends do."

"Friends don't get each other's cars impounded because they stashed their drugs in them."

"She paid to get the car back. It's not like it stayed in the impound lot forever."

"The car she borrowed from you."

This conversation was getting nowhere. Nobody seemed to understand Ryan's relationship with Ali, and very few people seemed to try.

"Why do you say Trey is too good for me?"

Mason dropped his cigarette on the ground and stepped on it, then picked it up and tossed it in the garbage can. "He's not the kind of guy you should be toying around with. He's— Ah shit, Ry. I can't talk about his business. I care about him a lot. Caro and I both do. You can't even decide if you're gay or straight. He doesn't need to be dragged into your identity crisis du jour."

"I'm neither. I'm not gay, and I'm not straight. It's pretty fucking simple. I'm bisexual. And you know what, Mason? *You* of all people should know what it's like."

Mason rolled his eyes and crossed his big arms over his chest. "I don't want to keep fighting with you. Keep your hands off the crew and your ass out of the papers, and maybe, just maybe, I'll forgive you for the heartache you've given your cousin."

"What about the heartache she's given me?" Ryan scowled. "You don't seem to mind that, do you?"

"You're a spoiled brat. One time in your life you didn't get what you wanted."

"I wanted my best friend to come to California with me. I wanted a new life for both of us."

"She didn't. She likes our life. And it didn't take you long to find a new best friend and flaunt her on the pages of every gossip rag and tabloid in the country."

"It's not like I *try* to get photographed by the paps."

"You didn't try very hard not to. Let's go. Time to read through act three."

Ryan was *wonderful*.

Trey watched with wide eyes as the actors read through their lines together for the very first time, bringing the story to a sort of half-life. Despite his youthful charm, Ryan managed to inhabit the role of Antony like a second skin. His voice rang out, and though he was seated, he tensed and arched his body with his words, portraying the type of dynamism he'd likely bring to the stage once they began blocking.

"Wow, he's really good," Trey whispered to Caro. "Is he even looking at the script?"

"He played Antony for the first time when he was sixteen. He loves this role."

"He was born for it."

Caro laughed. "I'm glad to hear other people recognize his talent. Before he got cast on that sci-fi show, I wondered if I only thought he was fabulous because he's my cousin and one of my best friends in the world."

"He's on TV? He's the guy I signed an NDA for?" Trey searched his memory for the name. "But the form said 'Bryan something.'"

"Yeah, Bryan Hart. That's his stage name. Ryan's his real name. So you mean to tell me you were having drinks with one of Hollyweird's most eligible bachelors, and you didn't even know it?"

He shook his head and watched as Ryan hissed out the words "You all did love him once" with such passion and anger that the building seemed to shake with it.

"I only watch sports. I'm a bro cliché."

"Explains why he likes you so much. He's used to people wanting to use him for his fame. If you didn't recognize him, he would have found it easier to relax with you."

Her statement caught him by utter surprise. "He likes me?"

"You couldn't tell? He doesn't flirt with just anybody. I mean, I can't say for sure, but you could probably totally hit that."

Trey had been lifting his water bottle to take a swig and jerked it away from his mouth before he could spew it across the room and embarrass them both. "Um."

"Oh my god, you did. You boned my cousin. Why does no one tell me *anything*?"

Trey slumped back in his seat. "He ran out of my house in such a hurry he forgot his pants. I don't think he found my performance as impressive as I find his Mark Antony."

"I am dying to hear his version of this story." Caro cackled. "Oh, I think you are exactly what he needs. But wait—what did he think of Ferdy?"

"Um. I didn't introduce them. We were busy, and Ferdy was out back when we got home."

Caro's eyes got huge. "Ryan is absolutely terrified of dogs. You've got your work cut out for you."

Trey glanced at the stage. Terrified of dogs? But Ferdinand had been in the living room that morning after, and Ryan hadn't said anything. He'd . . . *oops*. He'd just told Trey to keep his underwear. The yellow briefs Trey had found all chewed up in Ferdy's bed. *Oh hell.*

Chapter Four

Ryan's phone buzzed in his pocket during the read through, but he didn't get a chance to check his messages until they were done. Standing in the darkened hallway at the rear of the theater, he slid his phone from his pocket and read the text from Ali.

Hi, you. I'm doing better, just really brittle right now. I feel like I'm going to break and then I realize I already did, and this is what getting put back together feels like. Please don't stop texting. I'll answer when I can. I miss your voice. Leave me a voice mail sometime, okay? Say hi to West next time you see him.

He smiled and hit the Call button. When her voice mail picked up, his words poured out. "Hi, Al. I miss you. We did the read through of the first play today—have I ever mentioned how much I love *Julius Caesar*? Well, I do. Let's have a movie date and watch the Brando version when you get out. Movie marathons and then me cooking breakfast while you do whatever it is you do on your computer in the mornings. I love you. Be good. Don't break."

A clatter down the hallway made his head jerk up as he ended the call. "Who's there?"

"I'm sorry." The gravelly Savannah drawl brought a smile to Ryan's lips even before Trey stepped into the little circle of red light by the fire exit sign. "I was looking for you to apologize. I didn't mean to eavesdrop."

Trey was bigger than Ryan, with a work-hardened body and a sexy roll to his gait, but something about him reminded Ryan of a nervous horse. Ryan had once spent weeks on a farm, learning to ride for a film role that had mostly ended up on the cutting room floor. *His* horse had been a quiet brown and white mare with a longer list of production credits than he had—a real professional horse—but some of the others in the stable had been rescue animals, hand-shy and edgy. Trey moved with the same watchful care.

"It's okay. I was just leaving a voice mail for a friend. Why do you think you should apologize?"

"Do you tell all your friends you love them?" Trey's gaze skittered aside, like he didn't want to hear the answer.

Ryan realized then what it sounded like—like he was calling a lover. And he'd slept with Trey. "That was Ali. She's my best friend. And she needs to hear it a lot right now. I swear, I'm not an asshole."

Trey's face turned pink. "Caro told me you're scared of dogs. I'm sorry, I should have warned you about Ferdy before you fell asleep the other night. And I'm *really* sorry I called you an asshole. You didn't deserve that."

The gigantic beast was named Ferdy. "Oh. You mean his name's not Pork Chop or Killer or Grendel?"

"Killer?" Trey chuckled, and the sound triggered a sense memory for Ryan—hands skimming down his sides and spice in his mouth. "More like Cupcake or Kitten or Ludo—he's the biggest baby on the planet." He stepped closer, into Ryan's personal space. A big, callused hand cupped Ryan's jaw, thumb skimming across his lips. "I'm sorry he scared you."

Ryan's chest tightened as Trey's face filled his vision. Soft mouth quirking in a smile. That crooked nose and the mismatched ears. He bit his own lip to keep from groaning as blood rushed to his groin.

"Apology accepted," he murmured, stepping back, away from that achingly intimate touch, that big muscular body. He'd made a promise to Mason.

Trey's eyebrows pulled down in obvious confusion, then his face smoothed out. "Well. I guess I've said what I came here to say. We're going to be working together; I didn't want you to think I think you're an asshole."

"Okay." Ryan's heart pounded too fast in his chest. He wanted to grab Trey and haul him back against his body, taste those lips in rough kisses and feel those hands everywhere. "Um, good. I don't think you think I'm an asshole."

Trey laughed, but it didn't reach his eyes. "Good. I'll see you around, then."

As he walked away, Ryan watched the slow roll of his hips and ass and wondered how the hell he was going to keep his promise to Mason. He glanced down at his phone again. If only he could talk to Ali for real.

"There you are!" Caro came around the corner. "I'd almost forgotten how much you love this hallway."

Ryan smiled up at his cousin. "I will never live down that time you caught me kissing Katie Nixon back here, will I?" Never mind how he would have felt if Caro had caught him back here a few minutes earlier, with his promise to Mason inexorably breaking at the touch of Trey's hand on his jaw, thumb teasing, electric as a kiss.

"Well, you've grown up a lot since then. Come on, we need your measurements for costumes. We have togas and one-size-fits-all costumes from past shows that will work, but some stuff we're going to have to get new or have made."

"Gotcha." Ryan followed his cousin, taking one last peek over his shoulder at the red circle of light under the exit sign.

Trey and Caro were drawing up set plans with the lighting director, a petite, quiet woman named Viki, calling out for sandwiches at lunchtime and working straight through. By late in the afternoon, Trey was having trouble focusing. He wasn't artistic. Sure, he could build things, and he was good at visualizing what something *should* look like before it was done, but Viki and Caro were talking about shape and color and shadows in ways that went over his head. It was *exhausting*.

"We're losing him, Vik." Caro was half-sitting, half-sprawling across the stage floor, an open notebook in front of her. She kicked out at Trey's foot. "What are you thinking?"

I'm thinking that I should have kissed your cousin when I had the chance.

"It sounds good. The purple thing."

Viki laughed, a low chuckle. "I meant about setting it up so we can use the same sets for *Much Ado*."

He mulled it over. "They'd have to be pretty stripped down, but I don't see why we couldn't. We could put some pieces on wheels and . . ." Grabbing the sketchbook, he let his hand and pencil explain his vision for the sets, sketching it out in bold strokes.

Caro sat up and watched, nodding.

"Yes. Like a three-dimensional puzzle that can be reformed in different shapes. How much is it going to cost?"

"The lumber costs won't be much more than a regular set." He shrugged. "Hardware costs are going to depend on how many pieces we lock together. Good, locking wheels are absolutely vital. I don't know. I'll price it out and get you a quote."

"Give it to Mason. He's in charge of the budget." Caro glanced up toward the door to Mason's office, just visible through the curtains. A wistful little smile tilted her lips. "I'd better go see how he's doing. He wanted to cast *Much Ado* after seeing the first read through of *Julius Caesar*. If I know him, he's got Ryan's name penciled in at least four different places and he's trying to pick one."

"Ryan won't play Benedick?" He wasn't sure why he pictured Ryan in the romantic leading role, but he did.

"Oh, that would be an obvious choice, wouldn't it? But then David Wright would make a great Benedick, but he'd be lousy as either of the princes. Hasn't got the body language for it."

"He's going to cast Ryan as the villain?"

Caro considered it for a minute, then shook her head. "Don Pedro. But he's going think about Claudio awhile first."

"He'd be a terrible Claudio."

Caro laughed. "He'd be fine as Claudio. But he'll be excellent as Don Pedro."

"So David as Benedick, and Ryan as Don Pedro?"

The door to Mason's office opened, and he strolled out, face animated. "Caro? Would Ryan be better as Don John or as Claudio?"

Viki covered a snicker with her notebook, meeting Trey's eyes.

Mason stopped in front of them "Are those sandwiches?" He sat cross-legged on the floor next to Caro. "Can I have one?"

She gestured to the tray. "Whatever you want. But they're about two hours old."

"I don't care; I'm starving." He picked up a plate and a sandwich and started to eat, then dropped it back on the plate. "Not Claudio."

Caro smiled. "Nope."

"David could be Claudio, but I think he'd be a good Benedick." Mason's eyes went wide, and he clapped his hands together. "Don Pedro. Ryan should play Don Pedro. You don't think he'll be a diva about not getting the lead, do you?"

Viki snorted, her eyes pinched shut.

"Ryan has never minded not playing the lead. He'll be fine." Caro patted Mason's knee. "Don't you think so, Trey?"

"Yup." Trey nodded vigorously, Viki's hysterics sparking the devil on his shoulder. "Very fine."

Both the women laughed, and Mason shot him a suspicious glare. Oh shit, had Caro told him?

"I mean—"

"I know what you mean." Mason ground out the words. "I don't want any drama in my theater."

This time, it was Caro who hooted with laughter, leaning over and burying her face on Mason's shoulder until her own stopped shaking.

Trey grinned at Mason, shrugging. Mason had to know as well as anybody that blanket bans on hookups in the theater was an exercise in futility. Trey and Ryan were both grown men. And while Ryan had been the one to step away earlier, he hadn't seemed immune to the attraction between them. If Ryan was still interested? Well, Trey wasn't about to say no.

Chapter Five

Ryan laced up his running shoes at six thirty Tuesday morning with a grim reluctance. It had taken him too long to get back into a fitness routine since coming to North Carolina. Oh sure, he'd used the weights in West's home gym, but he hadn't bothered with cardio. And he needed to. His career required him to stay fit. Still, he didn't relish running under the summer sun any more than a monotonous slog on the dreadmill. He set the house alarm and then slipped out the back door, locked it, and jogged down to the deserted beach.

Despite the sweat and the sun, Ryan enjoyed running. Something about sinking into the perfect rhythm between breaths and steps was soothing. His mind could wander while his body worked. And he couldn't deny that the sunrise over the Atlantic was spectacular. If only he could share it with Ali—there had been lots of mornings in LA that had been the end of a drug-fueled night rather than the beginning of a new day. They'd greeted the dawn fumbling for their sunglasses and laughing as they stumbled into the house to sleep off whatever they'd taken. He didn't miss that lifestyle, not exactly. He missed the sense of raw excitement and the intimacy of his friendship with Ali. They'd shared everything—their career highs and lows, their home, their dreams. It was no wonder people thought they were in a relationship.

He didn't have that kind of closeness with anyone here, not even with Caro. Of course she was still family: his cousin, his best friend and surrogate mother. But hadn't she been the one to draw the line when he'd left for LA? Hadn't she been the one to choose renovating a decrepit theater with Mason over following Ryan's dreams to

Hollywood? So why did Mason think his friendship with Ali was hurting Caro?

A bark behind him pulled him up short. He turned to see Trey and his behemoth dog—Ferdy—playing in the surf. Trey lifted a hand, and Ryan circled back warily.

As Ryan approached, Trey gestured to the dog, who sank to sit on the sand, head cocked to one side. Ryan stopped a few yards away.

"Are you sure he's not going to eat me?" His heart fluttered in his chest, but Trey had called Ferdy a big baby.

"He's a gentle giant. He only eats underwear. Hold out your hand, let him sniff."

Ryan held out his hand, and the big beast lumbered to his feet and charged.

"Oh shit, he's huge." Ryan somehow managed to stand his ground as the dog shoved past his hands to sniff first his balls, then his running shoes. "He must weigh four hundred pounds."

"Less than half that. Ferdinand, come," Trey ordered, and the dog returned to his side. "See? Harmless."

"Why'd you name him Ferdinand?"

Trey scratched the dog's ears and grinned. "After the bull that would rather smell flowers than fight. It's a kids' book. Very subversive for its time."

"I've never heard of it. It doesn't sound like Dr. Seuss."

"No. Munro Leaf—he wrote it in the 1930s. People thought it was political commentary. It was banned and burned all over Europe. Fascism was on the rise and— I'm babbling, aren't I?" Trey glanced out at the ocean, then smiled shyly at Ryan. "I do that around good-looking guys."

Ryan blinked in surprise. Subversive kids' books banned in fascist countries? Trey's blue-collar exterior appeared to be hiding a closet historian. But why should he be surprised? What did he really know about Trey? Not much of anything. He vaguely remembered Trey saying his sister owned the beach bar where they'd met and drinking a toast to—what? A pregnancy? He wished he'd paid better attention, because the man standing before him was fascinating— and had just called him good-looking.

"No, it's cool. People don't tend to talk to me about stuff like this." Ryan smiled back and stepped closer, stroking the dog's ears. Ferdinand gave a low groan, dropped to the sand, and rolled until his belly was in the air. "I'll have to check this book out. I never thought of children's literature as potentially subversive. I like it."

"All literature is potentially subversive—sorry, my mom's a librarian. The political power of books is kind of a thing in our family."

"So your mom's a librarian. You're a contractor and part-time set designer. Your sister owns a tourist bar, and you moved here with your ex."

"Yeah, that about sums it up. Now you know everything about me." Something strained in Trey's voice made Ryan's smile falter.

"Sorry. I wasn't trying to be nosy. What did we talk about the night— Well. You know." Ryan grimaced, embarrassed. "I blacked out a lot of the evening."

"Mostly the karaoke singers. Who was good, who was bad. Then you put your hand on my thigh and said you were wondering if I tasted as good as the margaritas, and we didn't talk a whole lot after that."

Ryan threw his head back and laughed. "Really? I'm usually not that bold. In vino veritas."

"Or in tequila, testicles," Trey drawled.

Ryan laughed harder. "I hope nobody's testicles were in the tequila. Damn, I wish I remembered more. I bet it was fun."

"Jesus, Ryan. I didn't realize you were that drunk. God, I'm so sorry. I wouldn't have—"

Ryan flushed. "I didn't realize either—but I promise, I totally would still have gone home with you if I'd been sober."

"That doesn't exactly make me feel better. It's not like you could consent."

Ryan's heart thudded in his chest. They'd both been drunk. And he'd initiated it—hadn't he? Nausea rolled over him. Trey's face was hard to read, but the grimace twisting his lips looked just as bad as Ryan suddenly felt. If what had happened between them wasn't consensual— But he *had* wanted it. Wanting was the one thing he remembered clearly. He didn't know where the line was between being drunk enough to make the first move with a stranger and being too drunk to consent. He'd never had to think about this before, but he didn't want Trey believing Ryan had crossed that line, or that Trey had taken advantage.

"Believe me, I wanted it. Hell, Trey, you were drunk too. And I started it, so if anyone should be apologizing, it should be me. Please don't feel like—" he lifted his hands, helpless "—like you did something wrong. Yes, I was drunk. But I was into it."

"But I did—"

Ryan stepped closer, ignoring Ferdy snuffling at his leg, and wrapped an arm around Trey's waist. "Don't be upset with yourself, okay?" This was dangerously close to breaking his promise to Mason, but the thread of friendship between himself and Trey was so fragile—he didn't want that to break either.

Trey stiffened slightly, then his arms came around Ryan and his chin rested on Ryan's head for just a brief moment. He sighed and stepped back out of the hug. "Okay. But I'm not worried about me. I'm worried about you."

Ryan shook his head and buried his hands in his hair. "Don't. Please. Everyone worries about me. I don't need or want anyone else worrying about me. I was drunk, yes. But I promise, I wanted you."

At their feet, Ferdinand gave a low growl, and Ryan jumped back. "Are we okay?"

Trey reached down to soothe Ferdinand, and then he studied Ryan's face. "Are you asking about me or the dog?"

Ryan shrugged. "Both, I guess."

"If you're okay, we're okay. As for Ferdy—" Ferdy growled again, and Trey glanced around, then scowled "—there's a guy over in the dunes with a camera, and I don't think he's photographing the sunrise."

Ryan's heart sank as he surreptitiously peered over his shoulder. "Fuck, Mason is going to kill me."

"Mason?" Trey frowned. "Why?"

"It's a long, long story. Shit. I gotta go. It was great to see you—maybe I'll catch you out here again sometime."

"Sure, but do you need a ride somewhere?"

"Nah. Never met a pap who could run a six-minute mile with a camera to his eyeball. Later, Trey!"

Ryan heard a single low bark behind him as he took off toward the relative safety of West Brady's palatial beach house. How long would it take for more paparazzi to arrive? And how soon before his business was all over the tabloids? His sexual orientation, his exile during Ali's stint in rehab—none of it was anyone's business but his own. And one thing was for sure: if he kept getting himself photographed half-naked around Trey Donovan, the press was going to figure out he wasn't straight. And while he didn't really care who knew he liked to fuck guys, he'd rather it didn't come out while his name was still being linked romantically with Ali's by relentless gossips.

Some people might insist that Ali didn't need him to protect her, but his beautiful, outrageous best friend was fragile, and he couldn't be the straw to break her. He just couldn't.

Trey let Ferdinand into the house and dropped his leash on the table by the door, then pulled the door shut and locked it without following the dog inside. He'd promised Kim and Danny he'd help paint the nursery before he went over to the theater. There was about a one percent chance they actually needed his help, and a ninety-nine percent chance they were checking up on him, but either way, if he didn't show up, his sister would be pissed. And the number one rule in Donovan family relationships was that pregnant ladies got what they wanted. You could call that sexist bullshit, but Trey had three sisters and five nieces and nephews, and had seen plenty of pregnancy from the sidelines. Pregnant women deserved respect. And maybe a healthy dose of fear.

Kim threw the door open before he got up the steps, beaming at him. "I wasn't sure you'd come. How are you?"

"I'm fine." When he reached the top, he bent down to give her a hug. "How are you feeling?"

"Bloated, gassy—but that might be the baby moving around—and needing a nap before opening the bar, but other than that? I'm good."

"I'm glad."

"So, tell me about the hottie you went home with the other night."

"Oh my god. Is this why you wanted me to come over? So you could grill me about my sex life?"

She shrugged. "Old married ladies have to get their entertainment somehow."

"You aren't old, and he's one of Mason's summer stock guys."

"Oooh. An actor? Come on, I've got coffee brewing." She led him into the kitchen and sat him down with a steaming cup of black coffee. "Are you going to see him again?"

"I saw him this morning, actually. He goes running. Willingly."

"Without anybody chasing him? Dayum." She looked impressed. "What does Doc Wharton say?"

"About me or about my hookup?"

"In general. I know you had an appointment this week."

"She wants me to clean out the garage. By the way, she sends her congratulations."

"Awww. She's sweet. But Trey honey, you don't worry about the garage until you're good and ready. That stuff's not harming anyone just sitting there. Let it be."

Like he needed permission? He'd been letting it be ever since the divorce was finalized.

"Thanks. I think she's right though, you know? That I'll feel better with that stuff gone? But . . . Jesus, it's too much."

"If it's too much, it's too much. You don't recover on anyone's timetable but your own."

"Thanks, Kimmy."

"And if hard labor is good for the soul, there's a nursery upstairs that needs painting."

He wasn't sure about his soul, but working until his muscles ached was an excellent avoidance tactic. He swallowed down the rest of his coffee. "Lead the way."

Chapter Six

Summer stock rehearsal schedules could best be described as "grueling." The early morning calls for *Julius Caesar* were followed by afternoon calls for *Much Ado About Nothing*, each rehearsal often lasting four or five hours. By the end of the first week, everyone in the company was exhausted. Ryan was no stranger to the hard work involved in putting together a show, but by Friday afternoon when he arrived for the *Much Ado* rehearsal, he wanted nothing more than to go back to West's house, climb into the gigantic hot tub overlooking the beach, and let the aches and pains of performing on his feet for hours a day wash away.

"There's going to be a party on the beach tonight."

The voice startled Ryan out of his daydreams of salt-softened water and an early evening in. "Excuse me?"

David Wright was a bronze-skinned, curly-haired man in his early twenties with dark-rimmed glasses and a hipster beard. Ryan was eighty percent sure he was gay, and about fifteen percent sure he was *interested*. Sure enough, when Ryan looked up, David shoved his hands into his pockets, adopting a slouched nonchalance and a secretive smile. "The cast and crew are going down to the beach tonight, building a bonfire, and getting fucked the fuck up. I'm just letting you know in case you wanted to join us."

"Oh." Ryan was going to be working with this group for the next two months. This was the first party of what would probably be many among his castmates, so he was tempted to plead off—but David had mentioned the crew also.

Would Trey Donovan be there? Ryan hadn't talked to him since that day on the beach, but in the mornings when he arrived at the theater, new pieces had been added to the deceptively simple platforms and scaffolds that made up the ingenious sets Trey had designed. Every once in a while, the man himself would come into the theater and take measurements or deliver set pieces. He always had a quick nod for Ryan, but opportunities to chat hadn't come up. "Cast and crew you said?"

"Yeah. Donovan's sister is sending over a keg, and some of the guys who play music are bringing guitars and shit. It's going to be fun. Maybe you and I could grab a bite beforehand?"

And there it was. The invitation—the come on. Ryan wasn't in the habit of letting people down easy—wasn't in the habit of turning people down at all. He stared at David for a moment, tried to imagine kissing him, and squirmed. Yeah, he could imagine it, and it half turned him on. But he didn't *want* David, and he didn't want to say yes just because he couldn't figure out how to say no. Showing up to a party together was . . . way too public. Way too much of an *announcement*. If he was going to break his promise to Mason, he sure as hell wasn't going to do it with David Wright. The guy was hot, but so, for that matter, was Trey Donovan. And once his mind turned to Trey, there was no comparison.

"I'm sorry, I don't think that's a good idea."

"So it's true? You're straight?" David smirked now. "We all wondered."

"I'm not . . . anything. I don't date in the business. Not really." *Liar.*

"Hey, it's all good. I figured it was worth taking a shot." David shrugged. "I like finding a fuck buddy on my gigs. Keeps things uncomplicated. And you seem like an uncomplicated guy."

Ryan laughed in disbelief. "Jesus, David. You have no idea how wrong that is. I am nothing *but* complicated."

David grinned. "Ooh, you're definitely better off being someone else's problem, then. So, you going to the party or what?"

Thinking longingly of the hot tub and the early night he craved, Ryan sighed. Cast parties were as much a part of summer stock as the grueling rehearsals and early calls. And he was going to have to get used to being around his castmates socially. "Yeah, I'm going."

"Nice." David held his fist up for a bump, which Ryan gave with a smile he didn't feel.

"Thanks for letting me know about the party. No one else bothered."

"The others will loosen up around you soon. It's kind of weird, you not living in the short-term housing with the rest of us; it sets you apart, you know?"

Nodding, Ryan glanced around the theater at the other actors, who were gathered in groups and chatting. He hadn't attempted to make friends this first week, but it was clear that the others were forming fast friendships already. "Yeah."

"Well, if you need a wingman, let me know." David winked. "Gay men are chick magnets."

Ryan smiled in spite of himself. "So I hear."

"You aren't totally straight, are you?"

"Nope. What gave me away?"

"You get all twitchy and blushy whenever Donovan is around, and you stare at his ass like you've never seen one before."

"I do not."

"Okay, Hollywood, just keep telling yourself that."

Trey pulled his truck up behind the bar, and Danny wheeled the keg out on a little dolly and helped Trey hoist it into the truck. "Kim and I might come down to the party later, depending on how she's feeling."

Trey's brother-in-law was a nerdy, bookish man, deeply passionate about his hobbies—and his family. While his wife loved the social aspect of their business, he preferred to stay behind the scenes. A raucous cast party was not his idea of a good time, but if Kim wanted to go, Danny would be there. With Kim pregnant, Danny doted on her more than ever. Trey couldn't help but read between the lines of the *might* and the *depending* in that sentence and worry.

"Has she been sick?" Trey asked.

Danny shook his head. "She was in the first trimester. Now she's only tired a lot, and I can't get her out from behind that bar. She's a workaholic—I don't know what she's going to do when she gets too big to tie her bar apron."

"She'll go without." Trey loved his sister and was grateful that she and Danny had moved to Banker's Shoals to open their touristy pub and raise their family—it had brought them closer together at a time when he needed family most. But he didn't like the idea of his pregnant sister hauling herself out to a party to keep an eye on him.

"Well, here's your tap." Danny handed it over. "Enjoy. Maybe we'll see you later."

"Thanks, man. Give Kimmy a hug from me—and make her go home and put her feet up. I'll be fine."

Danny waved, and Trey climbed into his truck, butterflies in his stomach. He was glad for the distraction of setting up the keg when he first arrived at the party, because he didn't have to make small talk right away, and he could try to put his finger on the nervous anticipation tingling through his veins.

Trey wasn't watching for Ryan, not exactly, but when he caught sight of the actor's perfectly cleft chin and dazzling smile, something fluttered in his chest and his steps faltered. Ryan always looked good, but the sea air tousling his hair and the warm orange glow of firelight on his skin showed off his impish, playful side. Trey couldn't tear his eyes away.

Ryan glanced up, caught his eye, and raised a hand in greeting. Trey smiled and nodded back. Ryan had a small crowd around him, and Trey wasn't feeling particularly social, even though they were at a party, so instead of approaching, he sat while Ryan charmed his castmates.

And charm them he did.

Trey could only hear snippets of the conversation, but the parts he heard were good-natured anecdotes from Ryan's time in Hollywood. "One time, the casting agent asked if I could do a Scottish accent, and I *really* wanted the job, but . . ." And then the crowd roared with laughter as he launched into an appalling, exaggerated burr, and Trey found himself smiling along.

Eventually, though, Ryan separated himself from his admirers and made his way over to where Trey sat in a lawn chair at the very edge of the firelight. He carried a beer in each hand.

"Hi." This time, the charm was all for Trey, and the force of his response swept over him like a hurricane crashing on the dunes.

Trey swallowed and ducked his head. His face flushed with heat at the memory of Ryan in his bed—sweet and uninhibited and laughing. Tongue-tied, he gestured at the empty chair next to him.

Ryan's eyes widened in amusement as he sat down. "Wow. That's one hell of a line."

Trey laughed, and it loosened his tongue. "Shut up."

"Hey, somebody's gotta do the talking between us."

Between us. Trey's heart sped up in his chest. Friendly banter was a game for two. Ryan's hot-and-cold routine had been pretty hard to read, but finally, this was a cue Trey could follow.

"Is one of those beers mine?"

Ryan looked down at his hands and laughed ruefully. "Yeah, actually. I forgot I was holding them." He handed it over. "You have that effect on me."

"Nah. You're the one with all the charm. I saw how you were with the crowd." Trey took a long sip of the beer to cover his embarrassment. It was cold and bitter and just about perfect.

Ryan glanced up, his expression unreadable. "That's acting."

"I'm not talking about when you're on the stage. I mean—" Trey gestured at the actors dancing near the fire. "I mean, you're good in a group of people. They all like you, they all want to be like you. They envy you a little, but you're easy to be around and self-deprecating, so they admire you more than they envy you."

Ryan's lips quirked up in a very different kind of smile from the one he employed on the crowd. "Like I said. Acting."

"It's not just them." Trey tried again. "Caro and Mason worship you."

"Caro mothers me, and Mason barely tolerates me. He's a pretty good actor himself."

The bitterness in Ryan's tone took Trey by surprise. He glanced over at Mason, who, across the circle of firelight, was slow dancing with Caroline. Had there been any signs of tension between Mason and Ryan before? Now that he thought back . . .

"He has a tremendous amount of respect for you as an actor."

"And zero for me as a person." Ryan drained the rest of his beer in one big gulp. "Do you want to get out of here?" He stood up and extended a hand as if Trey needed help standing. And the gesture was too familiar, too close to one he'd seen before, that it tightened his chest, choking him.

Past and present clashed. Panic and reason chasing each other in circles. A helping hand reaching for him when he was beyond help. But no—he hadn't been. His chest hurt—was he dying?

No.

He was on the beach. At a party. Not in his kitchen. The bitter smell was beer, not blood. He glanced to his left, his right, naming the objects he saw nearby, forcing breath through his lungs and anchoring himself in the present.

Fire. Shoes. Sand. Guitar. Keg.

"Hey, man, are you okay? I just thought maybe we could walk down to the beach and get away from the heat and the crowd." Ryan's hand fell, and he squatted in front of Trey's chair. "You look like you saw a ghost."

Trey swallowed and took another swig of his beer to hide his shaking hands as Ryan's concerned eyes filled his vision. "I'll be okay. You reminded me of someone for a minute there."

"Oh yeah? Who?"

"Your cousin, actually."

"Caro? Someday you'll have to tell me what she did to put that look of terror on your face. She didn't pull some overprotective BS about us sleeping together, did she? 'Cause if she did—"

"No." Trey stood up. He had to shut this conversation down. "I'm sorry, a walk sounds great, but I have to get home to Ferdy."

"Oh." Ryan's face fell. "Got it. Well, it was nice to see you. Give Ferdy some ear scratches from me, okay?"

"Sure thing."

Trey's breath was still shallow and frantic-fast as he let himself into the truck and reached for the bottle of Xanax he kept in the console. Was this a full-blown panic attack? The rush of anxiety and the urge to dissociate often preceded one, but had he grounded himself in time? And if he took a pill, could he get home before it made driving dangerous?

He did the math in his head—the public beach access was a ten-minute drive from his place, and the drug usually didn't start making him sleepy until about thirty minutes after he took it.

As he sat there staring at the bottle, the passenger door opened, and Ryan climbed in. "I should have asked if you were okay to drive. How much have you had to drink?"

Startled, Trey looked up at him. "I'm fine. Only the one beer you brought me."

"You aren't acting like yourself."

Trey let out a short, mirthless laugh. "You don't know me."

Ryan nodded. "You're right, but I want to." He laid his hand on Trey's thigh, like he had the night at the bar, but tentative rather than bold. "This isn't a come on. I'm not trying to get you naked. I just— Caro is the only friend I've got here, and things are weird with Mason. My best friend is in rehab, so I can't even talk to her. I could use a friend, and I really like you, you know?"

Taking a long, slow breath, Trey fished a pill out of the bottle and swallowed it, then he handed Ryan his keys. "Take me home?"

Ryan smiled. "Of course."

Trey waited as Ryan walked around the truck, then he hopped down and held the driver's door open until Ryan was settled, then shut it gently. What the hell was he doing? He tried to quell the butterflies and nervousness in his stomach as he rounded the truck and opened the passenger door. He stopped dead.

Ryan was reading the label of his pill bottle.

He glanced up at Trey and shrugged. "Just curious as to what to expect when this kicks in. Ali used to take this sometimes, but the dosage wasn't as high."

Trey climbed into the truck and fastened his seat belt. "I'll get drowsy, but my heart rate will slow and I'll stop sweating and choking on nothing."

Ryan murmured an acknowledgment. "Anxiety attacks? That's rough."

He didn't know the half of it, and Trey had a hard enough time talking about it with his therapist, let alone a beautiful barely-more-than-stranger. Trey switched on the stereo. As country music filled the cab, Ryan started tapping his fingers on the steering wheel. "I turn left on Mustang, right?"

"Yeah." Curious about Ryan's familiarity with the island, Trey asked, "Did you grow up here?"

Ryan nodded. "Mostly. I mean, when I was little, we moved around some—lived on the mainland for a while. My aunt and uncle, Caro's folks, took me in when I was twelve."

"What happened to your parents?"

"The great state of North Carolina saw fit to remove me from their custody."

"Oh." Trey's mind reeled. "Jesus, I'm sorry."

Ryan glanced over at him. "I was a wild kid, and my dad was a control freak. He came to pick me up one day during one of their separations, I mouthed off, and he took a swing at me. It wasn't the first time, but this time *Mom* shoved him off the porch, he broke his ankle, and the neighbors called the cops. They got there just in time to hear my dear old dad tell my mom he was going to kill us both. It was ugly."

Trey shuddered. He knew all too well how ugly domestic violence scenes were when the cops got involved. But then, he knew exactly how ugly it was when no one came to the rescue either. "I'm so sorry."

Shrugging, Ryan stared at the road ahead. "It was a long time ago." But his voice was thick, and Trey knew bravado when he saw it. Some part of Ryan was still the wild, mouthy kid whose own dad took a swing at him, no matter how deeply he buried that kid under charm and swagger.

"Third one on the left." Trey pointed. "Thanks for driving me home."

"You're welcome." Ryan turned off the engine and handed over the keys. "My house—my buddy's house—is only about a mile and a half from here along the beach, so I can walk if you don't mind me cutting through your house to your beach access."

"I don't mind. Want a cup of coffee before you go?" Trey moved to get out of the car, but Ryan stopped him with a hand on his arm.

"How are you feeling?"

The company and the first lick of comfort from the Xanax had already started to calm him. "I'm going to be okay."

"Good."

Trey started up the steps to the front door of his little bungalow with Ryan trailing behind him. As he fit the key in the lock, he looked over his shoulder and Ryan was right there, so close, he could just—

"Trey?"

Damn, but his name looked good on Ryan's lips.

And suddenly all the dirty, dirty memories he'd been trying to hold back flashed through his mind at once. A laugh that became a moan. A fist in his hair. Teeth biting into his shoulder. His own name, over and over.

He pulled Ryan close, hands clutching desperately at the soft fabric of his T-shirt, and the promise of warm skin underneath.

"Not here," Ryan whispered, eyes wide in the dark.

Trey nodded, spun around, and fumbled with the key. Ryan's hand closed over his.

"I'm sorry."

"Don't be sorry." Ryan rotated Trey's shaking hand, and with it the key, and pushed open the door.

"Ferdy—"

Ryan guided him through the door and slammed it behind them.

"Is out back. I heard him bark when we pulled up." Ryan's voice sounded as breathless as Trey felt. "God, Trey, can we . . .?"

Trey turned, and their eyes met for just a moment before Ryan's hand came up and stroked Trey's ear—the ugly ear, the one he hated every time he saw it in the mirror—with infinite tenderness, sending a shudder rippling through him. Then Ryan's mouth was on his, lush and soft. Trey slid his hands around Ryan's waist, tugging them chest to chest and groaning as Ryan's teeth nipped his lower lip.

Ryan pulled back and smiled. "Even better than I imagined."

Trey took his hand and led him to the couch. He shoved Ryan down with a hand on his chest, then straddled his lap and drove his hands into that gorgeous golden-brown hair. This time, their lips came together hard and wild, hips rolling. Ryan's hands were everywhere—running down Trey's back to cup his ass, along his thighs and up to clutch at his waist, as if they could get closer.

We could.

But even as he thought it, Trey felt some of the tension seeping out of him and a warm fatigue weighing down his limbs. Ryan responded to the change in him by slowing the kiss as he deepened it, until he pulled away and Trey laid his head on Ryan's shoulder.

"I bet you're feeling relaxed after the Xanax and the beer, huh?" Ryan whispered. Trey nodded and took a deep breath. Ryan smelled like smoke from the fire, and like sweat from standing under stage lights, and just the smallest bit like grapefruit. He smiled into the curve of Ryan's neck and pressed his lips there.

"Oh god." Ryan's head fell back, and he thrust his hips, setting a ridiculously hot rhythm that ramped them both up. Trey nipped at a satiny earlobe and teased behind it with the tip of his tongue. Ryan had pretty ears.

"That's—oh—fuck, that's good."

He continued to explore the stubbled skin of Ryan's jaw and throat, listening to Ryan's breathy sounds of excitement, all the while rubbing their cocks together until they were both panting.

"Oh god, don't— Oh fuck, Trey, stop."

Trey reared back, dropping his hands to his sides. "I'm sorry."

"Don't be." Ryan smiled. "Please, don't be. But, dude. You're spacey and zoning out and after our talk on the beach the other morning..." He shrugged. "You gave me a lot to think about. And I meant what I said about us being friends, and maybe that means not fooling around when we're fucked up."

"I'm not—" Trey started, but Ryan's finger landed on his lips, and there was a finger on his lips so of course his tongue came out, and then Ryan laughed, and why was Trey giggling too?

"Yeah. You kind of are. That's a pretty high dosage of Xanax you're on. And you really shouldn't take it with beer."

"Yes, Mother," Trey teased, then nipped at the finger still on his lips.

"So, I'm going to tuck you into bed, and I'm going to let Ferdy in the house, and then I'm going to head home, okay?"

"Kay."

"So you gotta get off me." Ryan lifted his hips a little, and they both gasped as the movement brushed their cocks together. A fresh bolt of heat shot through Trey, and it took all the effort he had left to stand up and step away from Ryan. He pressed a hand against his aching cock and groaned.

"You're playing dirty. Come on." Ryan led him through the house to the bedroom and eased him down onto the bed. With a couple of quick tugs, Trey's Chuck Taylors hit the floor, then Ryan's hands were on his belt buckle.

"This okay?"

"Yeah," Trey rasped out. Ryan stripped him with gentle efficiency down to his underwear and T-shirt and somehow maneuvered him until he was stretched out under the blankets, head on his pillow.

"I'm going to let your dog in. Is he going to try to eat me?"

Trey smiled, then shook his head.

"Does he need anything?"

"Just make sure his water dish is full?"

"Sure. Gimme your phone."

"In my pants." Trey gestured to the pile of denim on the floor, and Ryan fished it out.

"Unlock it?"

"Why?"

"So I can put my number in it, goober."

Smiling, Trey held his thumb over the home button until his home screen appeared. A few moments later, his phone was locked again and sitting on the table next to his bed.

"Call me in the morning so I know you're okay." Ryan's lips brushed his forehead, and then he was gone.

Ryan pushed open the door to the backyard, heart pounding. "Ferdinand?"

A dark shape on the back deck made a rumbling sigh, then hefted itself to its feet and shook. Ferdy.

Ryan steeled himself against the wall as the giant gray dog lumbered inside, but Ferdy just gave him a brisk inspection of sniffs and snorts, then crossed to the mattress and lay down, tail thumping.

"Good boy," Ryan said softly. "You take care of your daddy, okay?"

The dog cocked his head to one side and yawned, and Ryan turned the lock, stepped outside, and pulled the door firmly closed behind him. Beach access for Trey's neighborhood was down a short communal path. The walkway was well lit and quiet, giving Ryan plenty of time to mull over what had happened at Trey's house. Two things were clear: his attraction to Trey was growing stronger, and he was going to have to tell Mason where he could shove his promise.

His phone buzzed in his pocket. He thought about silencing it without looking at the caller ID, but what if it was Trey? When he glanced at the phone, he had to do a double take. *West?*

"Hey!" he answered. "West, how are you?"

"Better question: *where* are you? I just got in and my house is empty. Thanks for leaving your cereal bowl in the sink, by the way. This is how we get ants." West's familiar Southern California accent was as comforting as a hug. Affection for his friend and anticipation swept over Ryan.

"Sorry. Won't happen again. I'm down on the beach walking home from a party. I'll be there in maybe twenty minutes."

West's voice shook with laughter. "I'm teasing you, Bry. I washed it and put it in the cupboard. I'm gonna open a bottle of wine and get in the hot tub. Join me when you get back; I miss your ugly face."

"I miss yours too." Ryan grinned so hard his cheeks hurt. "I'll see you soon."

He slid his phone into his pocket and kicked off his sandals, suddenly wanting to be back at the house *right freaking now*. Sandals in hand, he took off at a jog. He had so much he wanted to ask West. Had he talked to Ali? Did he know when she'd be out of the rehab program? What about the part they'd discussed before he'd come home to North Carolina? Was that project getting the green light?

By the time he unlocked the gate to West's backyard and jogged up the winding stone steps that led to the expansive patio, he was breathless with excitement and sweating with exertion. West waved from the hot tub, grinning in welcome.

"Come on in, I'll pour you a glass." West was classic Hollywood pretty, and had spent some time in front of the camera as a child actor. Now in his forties, his black curls were graying at the temples, but his blue eyes were full of the youthful sparkle that had made him a household name. He was one of the handsomest men Ryan knew, and it was easy to understand why Ali was so smitten with him.

"I'm, um . . ." *still a little turned on from making out with Trey.* "I'm just gonna grab my trunks from inside."

West threw his head back and laughed. "Dude, your dick's been in my mouth, I don't care if you get in the hot tub naked. Hell, I'm not wearing trunks either."

Blushing, Ryan turned away and stripped before climbing into the hot tub on the opposite side from West, who passed him a glass of something white and chilled, then clinked their glasses together.

They both spoke at once.

"Have you—" Ryan started.

"Has Ali—" West broke off with a laugh. "Go ahead."

Ryan took a sip of the wine. It was dry and crisp, just what he liked. "Have you talked to her?"

West's smile fell away. "Not since before she left for—for the spa. She came by the place all high and—" He shook his head. "We fought. We fought like we never fucking fought in five years. And then she grabbed my keys, left, and crashed my Benz. I haven't seen her since."

Ryan winced. "Sorry about the car, man."

Shrugging, West took a sip of wine. "I don't care about the goddamn car. I was pissed that she took it, because she could have gotten herself killed. But it's just a fucking car. I thought she'd learned her lesson after what happened with yours."

Not giving in to his natural urge to defend Ali—West was right, what she'd done was terrifying, and Ryan was every bit as pissed as West was—he just took a drink of his wine and closed his eyes.

They sat in silence for a long time, the steam and the hot water draining the tension out of them. Even though Ryan's boner was long gone, his mind was still half with Trey, wondering what had spurred the anxiety attack on the beach.

"So, have you talked to her?" West finally asked, drawing Ryan's thoughts back to the present.

"I got a text. I think she's committed to this recovery thing, but it's really hard for her. She told me to say hi to you."

"Yeah?" West glanced over at him. "Well, that's something." He sank deeper into the water and splashed some of it on his face and through his dark curls. When he spoke again, his voice came out raw and rough. "I can't watch her kill herself. Not after Jason."

The name stirred something in Ryan's memory. West didn't talk about his teenage years often, but he'd been famous, and there had been tabloid headlines when his costar had overdosed.

"Jason Fortune, right? You guys were—"

"Fucking dancing. I was dancing with my best friend in a club. And then he was gone. I can't watch her do that to herself, Bryan."

"*Ryan*. Here, on Banker's Shoals, I'm Ryan. And she won't. You have to believe in her."

West grabbed the bottle out of the ice bucket next to the hot tub and refilled their glasses, even though Ryan had barely sipped his. "She's in rehab. We'll see what happens next."

"You should text her. They let her check messages and stuff."

"I doubt she wants to hear from me after the way we left things."

"There is no one she'd rather hear from."

"Says you." West smiled. "Always the optimist. How is summer stock?"

Grateful for the subject change, Ryan shrugged. "Summer stock is weird. And . . . nostalgic too. I don't feel like I belong here most of the time, but then sometimes I'm saying one of Antony's lines and everything is so familiar it feels like I never left."

"Do you ever wish you hadn't?" West studied him intently from across the hot tub.

"No. I'm a perennial fuckup, but I'm acting for a living and I love it."

West nodded. "Good. Maybe now that you know how good you've got it, you'll stop fucking it up so much."

"Maybe." Ryan's thoughts flickered back to saying good night to Trey. "Maybe I already have."

"Do you have rehearsal tomorrow?"

Ryan shook his head. "No rehearsals on Saturdays. Thank god. Mason is a tyrant all week, but he doesn't own my weekends. I'm sleeping in."

"I'm here to scout some locations for a new project. Want to go for a drive?"

"Don't you have somebody to do that for you?"

West laughed. "Drive or scout locations?"

"Both."

"Yes. But sometimes I like doing things for myself like a grown-up. And seeing a location for the first time, it can help get the creative juices flowing, you know?"

Ryan had no idea. He wasn't creative the way West was—he created a character, lived in it, wore it like a second skin for the stage or the screen, but directing? Writing? That kind of creation mystified him. "I'd love to go with you."

They lingered in the hot tub, catching up until the wine was gone and the hour was late, but eventually their conversation dwindled, and when Ryan's chin nodded against his chest and he tasted saltwater, he knew it was time to say good night.

"I should go get a head start on that sleeping in." Ryan yawned theatrically, and it turned into a real yawn and they both laughed. He helped West cover the tub, and then followed his friend inside. As they started up the stairs, West turned to him suddenly, speaking fast.

"You don't have to sleep in the guest room, you know. You could sleep with me. We don't have to be alone."

Ryan's heart pounded in his chest as he stared at West. They both missed Ali, but West's loneliness was etched in every line of his face. And it was painful to see. Even though he was beautiful, kind, and brilliant, Ryan didn't want him.

"I'm sorry, West. We've had fun in the past, but it doesn't feel right anymore."

"Ali wouldn't mind—she'd probably like to know we were . . ." West bit his lip, then leered. "Taking care of each other."

Ryan ran a frustrated hand through his hair. "I think she would mind, actually. But that's not really the point. Please don't make this weird, dude."

West smiled mournfully and nodded. "I'm sorry, Bry. I didn't mean— Well. I did. But let's just forget I said it, okay? We still on for the road trip tomorrow?"

"Yeah. Not until after noon though. I'm sleeping in!"

Chapter Seven

Trey woke up with a start in the early hours of the morning when Ferdinand put his chin on the bed and whined.

"Hey, Peanut," he murmured, moving over to make room and throwing a hand across his eyes. "Come on up."

The dog heaved his bulk onto the bed and settled next to him with a satisfied grunt. A few minutes later, he was snoring, feet twitching.

Trey, on the other hand, was wide-awake, the memory of Ryan's kisses running hot on his skin like physical touch. Wide-awake, sober, and absurdly grateful that Ryan had put a stop to their make-out session. He wanted Ryan, wanted him more than he could remember wanting anyone in years, but he knew better than to try to bury his anxiety in another person's body. A few moments, a rush of pleasure—but the panic would inevitably return, this time with a side heaping of guilt.

Still. Fooling around with Ryan had been fun. And this time, Ryan had left his number.

He found his phone on the table next to the bed and opened his contacts. There was Ryan's face, grinning back at him in low light. Gorgeous. Even the phone camera had managed to capture that mischievous, carefree expression that Ryan always seemed to wear, the one that made Trey feel like they were sharing the best joke ever.

Thanks for taking care of me last night.

He typed out the text, thought about deleting it, then hit Send before he could change his mind. When the phone buzzed a few minutes later, he was drifting back into a pleasant doze.

Anytime. What are you doing up so early?

Ferdy.

That dog is a sadistic monster.

Chicken. He's a big baby who wanted some snuggles. What are you doing up so early?

He waited for what seemed like an eternity for a response. When it finally came, it brought a smile to his lips.

Nothing could get me out of bed this early but a text from you. Actually, I'm still in bed. Wish you were here.

A flush heated Trey's face, and he dropped the phone on the bed. He wanted to self-deprecate. He wanted to demur, make a joke. The idea of having Ryan's attention like that—he hadn't recognized since that first morning when Ryan had snuck away how much he had wanted it. Not the drunk, laughing, spirited Ryan he'd taken to bed, but Ryan sober and still wanting him was something he barely let himself hope for. Ryan's rejection that morning had stung deeper than he realized. How long had it been since he'd felt really, truly wanted? And yeah, maybe Ryan was playing him—he was an excellent actor— but right now? With those flirtatious words on his phone screen, Trey didn't give a fuck—it felt good to be wanted.

He picked the phone back up.

What would you do with me if I was?

Ryan stared at his phone. Was this really happening? Was he going to do this? His publicist had told him time and again to never put anything in writing that he wouldn't want on the front page of a tabloid, but did text messages count?

I'd like it better if you did me.

It was frank, and it could be publicly humiliating if text messages did count. But Ryan instinctively trusted Trey, not just with his body, but with his reputation, or whatever was left of it.

I'd kiss you for hours.

The text brought a smile to his face. He loved the way Trey kissed—like it was his favorite thing ever. Like he had all the time in the world to get it just right, and he intended to take it. *Just kiss? Really?*

No. But that's where it would start. You laugh when you kiss. It's cute. And when I kiss that spot behind your ear, it makes you wriggle and you make the hottest sound. I think about that sound a lot.

Ryan's breath hitched, caught in his throat, and then bubbled out in a laugh as he wondered whether that was exactly what Trey had meant. He was hard as a rock now, his dick tenting the soft sheets. Even though he had been planning to sleep in, this was a million times better.

You have an advantage over me, with your superior memory. Remind me?

He palmed his cock through his briefs, letting the fantasy wash over him. Trey's lips on his throat, Trey's hands on his body.

The next text included a picture. The muscles of Trey's chest and abs were covered with a light dusting of strawberry-blond hair and freckles. His lips were curved in a wicked smile, the tip of his tongue just visible between his teeth. At the edge of his boxers, a tiny tattoo caught Ryan's eye. He wanted to put his mouth on it. Kiss it, bite it. He groaned and squeezed his dick harder. His phone buzzed again.

Did that jog your memory?

Fuck this. Kicking the sheet away, he hit the FaceTime button and waited for the call to connect. What if Trey didn't answer? What if he was fine with texting but not video? Who knew sexting could be fraught with anxieties that drunken hookups weren't?

When Trey's face filled the screen a moment later, an absurd wave of relief and renewed desire hit Ryan.

"Hi," he whispered.

"Hi, yourself." Trey's voice was a little breathless. "I mean, good morning."

"Good morning." Ryan laughed. "Is this okay? God, you're pretty."

Trey made a face. "Pretty? Me?"

"Yeah." Ryan nodded. "I can't wait to get my hands on that chest. Touch it for me?"

"Like this?" Trey tilted the phone so Ryan could watch as he caressed his own pecs, tugged at a nipple, pinching and rolling it between his thumb and forefinger. Ryan imagined those work-roughened hands on his own chest and let out a low moan. His screen filled with Trey's face again. "Your turn."

It took a minute, but Ryan found a way to prop his phone up on the table next to the bed so that most of his body showed. He ran one hand over his chest and cupped his cock with the other. He flicked at a nipple, shuddering as it tightened.

"Nice," Trey murmured, voice strained. "Take your briefs off, I want to see your cock."

Ryan scrambled out of his briefs and tossed them on the floor, then grabbed his dick and gave it a long, slow stroke.

"Do you ever play with your ass when you jerk off?"

Oh *god*. He bit his lip and nodded. "I love it. Love ass play. Fuck, Trey, I'm so turned on."

Trey let out a rumbling, humming sigh. "Mmm. Me too." On the screen, Trey's dick filled the frame, and it looked wet—was that lube? Spit? Pre-come? Ryan didn't know, didn't care. It was hot as fuck, and he squirmed.

"Is that for me?" he teased, his mouth watering as Trey's hand slid over the head, squeezing a little drop from the end.

"Yeah. Just for you, Ry. I want you to suck it, get it nice and wet."

Ryan shoved two of his fingers in his mouth and sucked, wishing they were Trey's cock. He loved giving head—loved getting it too, who didn't? But right now, he wanted to give Trey a show, sliding slick fingers in and out of his mouth.

"That's good. That's really good. Now roll over."

Ryan turned onto his stomach and thrust his dick against the sheets, still sucking on his fingers. He loved the sensation of his mouth being filled almost as much as he loved the vulnerability of turning his back to the camera.

"I'd love to see you up on your knees. Will you show me your ass?"

Ryan pulled his knees up under him, but left his chest pressed to the mattress. He couldn't see Trey anymore, not with his reddened face pushed into the pillow, but just hearing his voice was enough. Especially when he was giving orders. Ryan loved bottoming, but even more, he loved being topped. Having a guy tell him what to do, making him wait for it—it made him crazy. He wasn't into kinky shit or anything, he just liked guys who were bossy in bed.

"Show me where you want my dick."

Ryan groaned and reached back with his spit-slick fingers to probe at his own ass, sliding one fingertip in and letting out a gasp.

"Push it all the way in. Can you take two?"

Nodding frantically, Ryan shoved both fingers in, loving the stretch, and loving Trey's perceptive, toppy nature.

"Grab your dick with your other hand and jerk it while you fuck yourself."

If he did that, he was going to come. The orgasm welled up in him before he even touched his cock, but a few strokes with his fingers in his ass were all it was going to take.

"I'm going to come," he warned.

Trey's throaty laugh filled the room. "Yeah, me too. God, you're sexy. Roll onto your side so I can see your face."

It was awkward, with his fingers still in his ass, but Ryan managed to do as he was told and then grabbed his dick as he thrust his fingers deeper. He opened his eyes and looked up to see Trey's face filling the screen, teeth digging into those beautiful lips, and that tipped him over the edge, sending the orgasm rushing through him.

"Oh *fuck*." His body shook with the force of it, and he pulled his fingers out of his ass and bit down on the heel of his hand to keep from shouting as he spurted all over his chest and belly.

He heard a guttural groan, and his iPhone showed Trey's mouth open, eyes closed tightly in ecstasy, a ruddy flush across his cheekbones.

As the tension seeped out of his body, Ryan grabbed a T-shirt off the floor and mopped at his chest, then gave up and stared at the screen, where Trey was staring back at him, breathing like he'd just run for miles.

"That was—"

"Fucking incredible," Trey finished for him. "You're amazing. I want to kiss you so bad right now."

Ryan's eyes drifted closed, and he bit his lip as his dick gave another jerk. "God, yeah. Even after coming like that, I want you."

At a muffled noise from the phone, Ryan looked up. Trey was gone.

"Are you still there?" he called. "Was it something I said?"

"Yeah, still here." Trey's face reappeared. "I'm sorry. I kicked the dog out of the room when the texting turned dirty, and he was whining at the door."

"I'm so glad you texted this morning. That was fun—I've never done that before."

"Sexting or the FaceTime?"

"Either," he confessed. "You make me reckless."

"How is it a guy who has a reputation as a Hollywood playboy has never had text sex?"

Ryan flinched at the reminder of his slutty reputation. Did Trey believe everything that was said about Ryan? And why did Ryan care if he did? He wasn't ashamed of enjoying sex. He took a deep breath and pulled on his best nonchalant smile to cover the sting. "Moviemaking doesn't leave a lot of time for relationships, and believe it or not, I don't just hand out my phone number to every hot person I meet. And even if I did, so what?"

So much for nonchalance.

"Hey, I didn't mean . . ." Trey's face flushed with embarrassment. "I didn't mean it like that. Ryan, please—"

"My friend West is in town, and we're driving down the coast today, maybe taking the ferry to the mainland, so I'm gonna go now. Thanks for popping my sexting cherry."

Ryan disconnected the call and tossed the phone on the bed.

Yeah, he totally sucked at nonchalance.

Chapter Eight

Ryan made his way down to the kitchen and found West pouring himself a big cup of coffee.

"Good morning."

West looked up and gave him a sheepish grin. "Hi. Can I just say I'm sorry for making a pass at you last night so we can spare ourselves the awkward and move on?"

Ryan stared down at his shoes. This was good, right? "Yeah, bro. Already forgotten."

"Thanks. So, what happened to sleeping in?" West poured a second cup—black—and handed it over to Ryan, then grabbed Ryan's box of Grape Nuts out of the cupboard and made a face. "I can't believe you eat these."

"Yeah, well, I have to maintain my girlish figure. There's bread in the pantry and eggs in the fridge if you want to make French toast or something."

"Or we could grab breakfast on the road? Surely you can get something healthy somewhere along the coast? I mean . . . since you didn't sleep in after all . . ." West wheedled.

Ryan took a sip of his coffee and rubbed his eyes. "Okay. Lemme go put some deodorant on and find my sandals."

An hour later, they were cruising down Highway 12 in West's Ferrari, wind whipping their hair and West's favorite nineties music blasting from the speakers.

"Are those horses?" West pointed at the shoreline.

"Yeah. There are maybe fifty or seventy-five of them here on Banker's Shoals. More on Corolla."

"Wow. Okay, good to know. How far are we from Wilmington?"

Ryan side-eyed his friend. "Like five hours. You want to go to Wilmington today?"

"No. But there's a decent-sized film industry there. Lots of union people. Big sound stages."

"You've talked about making a movie out here before, when you bought the house. You got a script yet?" Ryan bit back the question he really wanted to ask. *Is there a role for me?*

"It's not a movie. I'm shooting a pilot out here. Ali . . . Ali and I wrote the script together."

Ali? *His* Ali wrote a pilot script? Suddenly all the times he'd seen her hunched over her laptop chugging coffee instead of sleeping off a hangover made a lot more sense.

"Holy shit. She never said anything. Is it— It's a done deal? The pilot is happening?" Ryan was giddy and breathless at the thought of what this meant for Ali. A writing credit. A chance to show she was more than the pretty face with devilish comic timing.

"The pilot has gotten the greenlight—I'm going to be funding a lot of it myself. If the season gets picked up . . ." He shrugged. "I had this idea of living out here for a few years. Getting away from the noise and the stink and the parties. That was back when Ali and I were still together though. Then there was the accident, and now she's in rehab, and who knows what's going to happen next."

Ryan swallowed and stared at the blue coastline whizzing past. "Do you still want that?"

West shrugged again. "I suppose it depends on a lot of things. One step at a time, you know? But I can see it—opening credits with the wild horses even. Can't you picture it?"

"Sure." But Ryan couldn't. This was the home he'd rushed to escape from. Who would want to watch a TV show about it? Looking out at the ocean and feeling the wind in his hair, he remembered curling up under the boardwalk with Caro and Mason like so many puppies and sharing their dreams of acting—how was he supposed to know back then that he was the only one who actually wanted to leave? But there had been moments when he'd wanted to stay frozen right there with the only people in the world who loved him.

"You still with me?" West put his hand on Ryan's knee, shaking him out of his nostalgia.

"Yeah. Sorry. Can I ask you something?"

"Of course."

"Do you think I'm a slut? I mean . . . I don't know. I know I have a *reputation*. In the tabloids or whatever."

West growled. Honest to god, like an angry dog, *growled*. "Fuck your reputation. *Slut* is a word used to shame people who are having good sex—usually women, but sometimes us homos too. You never gave a fuck what people thought about you and Ali back in Hollywood. Are people here making you feel like shit because you had fun out there?"

Ryan shook his head. "Not exactly. I got mad at—at a friend this morning. What he said wasn't that bad, but . . . I guess I'm just sensitive about it. I don't know how to deal with what people here think of me, on top of what I feel about what I've done or haven't. And the fucking press—my ass was on the front page of the paper. I can't even."

West grimaced. "Dude. I have so been there—not my ass on the front page, but figuring out the sex stuff. But that's part of what this summer was for, right? Introspection? Getting away from the toxic scene?"

"Hiding out at home while my best friend is in rehab?"

"Do you need to be in there with her?"

Ryan shook his head. "I smoked weed. I drank a lot. The one time I smoked opium, it made me itchy, so I never tried heroin. And coke was good, but I only did it when Ali had some at the house."

"You don't have to be addicted to something to depend on it."

"I don't feel like I need those things—and I know there are fancy words for all the ways Ali and I fucked each other's lives up—"

"It's called codependency."

"Yeah, that. But I was in it for her. Not for the drugs. With her, and the parties, I knew who I was. I was the party guy. I was having a good goddamn time. And I don't know who I am if I'm not the party guy."

"I know what you mean." West ran a hand through his hair and smiled over at Ryan. "Being young and hip in Hollywood is . . . intoxicating. But I went through an identity crisis when Jase died.

He was—he was like Ali, a lot. And I partied with him, but . . . then when he was gone, who was left? I didn't want to party without him, but I didn't know what else to do with myself either. And I didn't have a theater back home to find myself in because I grew up under cameras."

"Caro and Mason have been really good to me."

"Have they? 'Cause here we are, driving down one of the most gorgeous highways in the country in a goddamn Ferrari, and you're queening out about your reputation like you're worried that sleeping with the captain of the football team will ruin your chances to pledge Delta Cannot Help Ya next fall."

"Did you learn everything you know about high school from John Hughes movies?"

"Yes." West laughed. "The joys of growing up on movie sets."

Well, that explained a lot, actually. "But don't you feel weird, like there's two different worlds, and we have to live in both of them?"

"I've only ever lived in one world, Bry. I make prettier, funnier facsimiles of the other one for money. You know what your problem is?"

Oh, great. Why was everyone so damned eager to tell him what was wrong with him? "No, what?"

"You don't believe anything about yourself unless it's been said by someone else. You don't trust your talent, and you want other people to validate your choices. You crave approval but settle for attention."

Ouch. "You make me sound like a toddler."

West shrugged. "If the shoe fits."

"That's not fucking fair. You have no idea what it was like for me—" Ryan choked on his own words. He didn't talk about his childhood. Why would he? Why would he want to talk about a dad who hit whatever and whoever disagreed with him or got in his way? A mom who hit back? The constant fighting over everything from money to the yardwork and housework that had never seemed to get done, no matter how much they screamed at each other? The sarcasm and ridicule whenever he did something wrong? "You don't know what I went through."

"No, I don't. And I have empathy for you, dude, I so do. But here's my world: My world doesn't care whether you find yourself or not.

It doesn't care what you've overcome, because there are thousands of fuckers out there who want your job and are just as pretty as you. All anyone cares about is whether you can show up on time, do your fucking job, and whether your name can sell the fucking movie. I'm out here to work. What the fuck are you doing?"

"I'm working!" Ryan exploded. "Theater is serious acting too."

"Your name isn't in lights on Broadway, Ry. You're playing secondary roles in a seaside playhouse in North Carolina."

"I'm *working*. It's real acting. Small-town summer stock theaters are important—they're part of the local tourist economy. They provide jobs. And let's not forget—as long as I'm here, nobody is writing tabloid stories about me and drugs and sex. The story, so far, is just that I'm here. Okay, yeah, so what. I'm fucking here."

"So be here. Get what you're going to get out of being here. But if you come back to LA, to the microscope and the high pressure of a film set, and the tabloids are writing about your dick or what you put up your nose? Dude. Welcome to the D-list."

Trey let himself into the theater and stopped short when he heard voices from the office. Mason and Caro never worked Sundays, but there they were. And it sounded like they were arguing.

"Hello?" he called, to warn them he was there. A moment later, Caro came out of the office, her face flushed and her eyes red, ringed with smudged mascara. She pushed past him like he wasn't even there, and before he could stop himself, he grabbed her arm.

"What's going on, Caro?"

"Nothing. Come on, I'll help with the sets."

"You're the stage manager, not one of my crew."

"Doesn't matter, it needs done."

So Trey dropped his iPod into the sound system dock, put on his favorite playlist, and they began turning the plywood set pieces into stone walls and stairs. He liked painting—liked seeing the sets come to life under his hands. He liked the mess and the smell. He found the work soothing, and when he got into the rhythm of it, time seemed to fly.

Caro attacked the work with a ferocity he rarely saw from her, periodically shoving her wild hair out of her eyes and sniffling loudly. "Have you got a rubber band somewhere?" she finally demanded. "My hair band broke."

"No, but I've got a bandanna in the truck." He pulled his keys out of his pocket and handed them over. "It's in the console. Should be clean. If you want to sit out there and freshen up your makeup, there are baby wipes in the glove box. I won't tell."

She looked up at him sharply. "It's not what you're thinking."

Trey sighed. He'd seen Caro and Mason dance around each other at work for years. Their relationship was more or less an open secret—anyone with eyes could see they breathed each other like air. He'd never met two people who complemented each other so well. In the theater, they were always professional—and they had never openly acknowledged their relationship to their employees. If he'd known he was going to interrupt a lovers quarrel, he'd have left them to sort it out. Still, he couldn't bring himself to say it in those words. Their relationship had been the elephant on the stage for as long as he'd worked in the theater. Everyone pretty much knew, but no one talked about it.

"What am I thinking?" he asked instead.

"The business is not going under. It's *not*." She wiped her eyes and set her chin. "I'll be back."

Well, hell. He hadn't been thinking anything like that. Shakespeare by the Sea in financial trouble? Like most of the island's small businesses—like his *own*—the theater depended on tourism to stay solvent. Unlike his own business, however, they had the bellwether of advance ticket sales to indicate how the season would go before it even started. If they were in trouble, what did that mean for the rest of the island?

Trey set his paintbrush down and made his way to the office. Mason had his laptop open, but was staring off to the side, a blank expression on his face.

"Hey, buddy," Trey said softly. "How's things?"

Mason looked up and scrubbed a hand over his face. "Fine."

"Caro seems pretty upset."

Mason grunted. "She's so goddamn pigheaded about that cousin of hers."

Trey flushed, wondering how much Mason knew, and how his own involvement with Ryan would go over with his boss. "How do you mean?"

Mason shoved away from his desk, chair wheels squealing. "Walk with me, I need a smoke."

They walked in the dark through the hallway encircling the stage to the exit sign by the back stairs, the exit sign that made Trey think of Ryan's lips dropping open in surprise when Trey had apologized for Ferdy. *God, Ryan.* What was he going to do about Ryan?

"So, this thing with Ryan is complicated."

Trey blinked, and Mason took a long drag on his cigarette before he continued.

"Caro doesn't want to advertise that Bryan Hart himself is part of our company because she's afraid it will bring unwanted attention. But Bryan Hart's name could sell tickets, and our cash flow is down."

"Unwanted attention?"

"Paparazzi."

"He's already got photographers stalking him," Trey pointed out. "How much worse could it be?"

Mason shook his head. "Worse. Trust me. But the kid brings it upon himself; I don't see why I need to protect him."

"Have you asked *him*?"

"She won't let me. She thinks it could damage his career if too much attention is drawn to him doing community theater." Mason made a face, then offered a perfect mimicry of Caro's lilting voice. "It's not like it was back in the sixties when it was trendy to do summer stock."

"I get that he's *her* cousin, but it's *your* theater too."

"Yeah, well. They're close." Mason plastered the fakest smile Trey had ever seen across his face. "I appreciate your concern, I do, but Caro's right: we'll find a way without advertising he's here."

"I didn't realize it was that bad, Mason. I'm sorry."

"It's not. It's just— It's summer stock Shakespeare. Money is tight is all. We'll get through. We always do."

"What would you and Caro do if . . . if you don't get through? Would you ask him then?"

Sighing, Mason stubbed out his cigarette. "I don't know. I've spent a decade and change trying to figure out why she lets him run wild over what she wants."

"She loves him. Family is . . ." Trey thought about what Ryan had let slip about his family the other night. "Family is complicated."

"Yeah." Mason glanced over at Trey as he lit another cigarette. "I'm sorry. I'm not good company right now. Is there anything else?"

Trey shook his head and then, dismissed, returned inside.

He stopped dead at the edge of the round stage, his body flushing hot with surprise and shame. Caro had returned, mascara-smudges gone and hair held back by his bandanna, and Ryan had joined her, taking up a paintbrush to paint the stairs. What was he doing here? Was he still mad about Trey's stupid, thoughtless comment? God, Trey would give anything to have never spoken those words.

Ryan was dressed in faded khaki shorts and an old ratty T-shirt with more holes than a cheese grater. When he saw Trey, he gave a shy grin and awkward wave. His grin was infectious, and Trey smiled back.

"You're painting sets now? Is this a Hertzog thing? No job too small?"

"I called Caro to see if she wanted to get brunch, and she said she was here." He dipped his brush in the bucket, carefully wiping it to keep it from dripping on the stage floor. "So, here I am, just like old times, right Care?"

"Yup. And he brought doughnuts like a regular fucking hero. They're in the booth if you want one." She gestured with her paintbrush.

"Oh, awesome. Thanks, Ryan."

"You're welcome."

Trey made his way to the control booth and the box of doughnuts sitting there. He grabbed a blueberry-cake doughnut and took a huge bite. He almost groaned with pleasure as the sweetness burst across his tongue. Two bites later, the doughnut was gone and he was licking glaze off his fingers as he walked back to the stage.

"Did you go to that new place on the boardwalk?" he asked around his thumb.

"I did. My old chemistry teacher owns that place. They're pretty great, yeah?" Ryan grinned.

"Amazing. That blueberry-cake doughnut was practically orgasmic."

Caro snorted but said nothing. Her mood had visibly improved with her cousin's presence.

Trey picked up his brush and got back to work, stealing peeks here and there at Ryan, who had started at the bottom of the stairs and was painting his way up. He would be in for a rude awakening when he got to the balcony and found himself trapped up there until the paint dried.

"Hey, Ryan?" he began, but Caro caught his eye and shook her head, her own eyes twinkling with mischief.

"What's up?" Ryan glanced over his shoulder expectantly.

"Oh, I was just going to ask if you would prefer to listen to something else? Or is this music okay?"

Ryan shrugged and sang a few lines along with the pop music pouring out of the sound system. "Nah, this is good, thanks though."

Caro covered her laugh with a cough and started singing along with Ryan, and before Trey knew it, they had broken into harmony and he was humming along.

They worked for an hour before Caro seemed to have burned off enough of her anger to go back to the office with Mason, leaving Trey and Ryan alone.

"Hey," Ryan said softly, and Trey looked up. Ryan had stopped painting and was leaning over the banister flanking the stairs and smiling.

"Hey, yourself."

"You work every day?"

"I work when there's work, same as everyone else. Listen, I'm so sorry about yesterday—I don't think of you that way. It wasn't fair of me."

"It's okay." Ryan shrugged. "It's nothing I haven't brought on myself. I do have a reputation as a playboy, party animal. Worse. You're only seeing the face I showed the world."

"I really *don't* think of you that way. It was a stupid thing to say."

"Thanks." Ryan gave a wry smile. "I appreciate the apology."

"Hey. I wouldn't say it if I didn't mean it."

That seemed to satisfy Ryan for a while, and they worked in companionable silence, occasionally singing along with the music, until Ryan, now at the top of the stairs, muttered, "Fuck."

Trey looked up, feigning concern. "Something wrong?"

"I started at the bottom."

"Yup."

"I'm stuck."

Trey grinned. "Yup."

"You *knew* this was going to happen?" The outrage in Ryan's voice was priceless.

"Maybe."

"Why didn't you say anything?"

From the office, Caro howled with laughter.

"Oh, that bitch."

"She's *your* cousin."

Caro and Mason came out of the office to the stage. Clearly the morning's argument had abated, and they were back to normal—or faking it for Ryan's benefit. Mason's eyebrow lifted, and he shoved his hands in his pockets, scanning slowly up and down the staircase.

"Well, you seem to be in a bit of a pickle."

"Shut up." Ryan glowered. "It's not funny."

"Mason and I are going to go." Caro took Mason's arm. "We'll see you Monday, Ry."

"You're just going to leave me here?"

"I'll keep you company." Trey smiled up at him.

"Whoa, wait—" Mason stopped in his tracks.

"You promised, Mason. Come on." Caro gave Mason's arm a tug. "Bye, Trey, Ryan."

Ryan shot her the bird.

Their laughter was audible on stage until the front door of the theater swung shut behind them.

"Mason doesn't want us hooking up." Ryan spoke so matter-of-factly, it cut off Trey's own laughter. His jaw dropped open.

"What does that mean?"

"It means . . . I don't know. I need to talk to him, because he told me to keep my hands off the cast and crew. And I promised him. Shit.

I told you he doesn't respect me?" Ryan sat down on the balcony and crossed his legs, looking at Trey expectantly.

"Yeah, but I think you're wrong about that."

"This is part of it. He doesn't think I'm good enough for you. He judges me without having walked a minute, much less a mile in my shoes. He thinks I'm a fuckup, and he only grudgingly allowed me to come join the company this summer."

Trey's mind reeled at that. Ryan not good enough for *him*? Someone's wires were crossed somewhere. "So, you let your director dictate who you sleep with?"

"No! It's not that. You just have to understand. Mason is like . . . He's the reason I started acting. He was the first guy I ever had a crush on—and, oh boy, that did not go well—and over the years he's become like a stern older brother I've been trying to impress. But all I did was make him think less of me."

Ryan bit his lip and looked up at the stage lights, and Trey wanted to climb up onto that balcony, wet paint be damned, grab his shoulders, shake him, and tell him that he was more than enough just as he was.

"I want to be the kind of guy Mason thinks you deserve." Ryan shrugged. "Because I really fucking like you."

Trey slipped off his shoes and set them aside.

"What are you doing?" Ryan asked.

"Coming up there with you."

"You'll get paint on your feet!"

"They'll wash."

The paint was tacky rather than wet, but it did stick to his feet. He didn't care. He was dressed for painting—and they would wash. Whatever was going on in Ryan's head that had brought him so low— that wouldn't wash. That could only be rebuilt over time.

At the top of the balcony, Ryan stood with his arms folded over his chest, stone-faced.

Trey stopped at the top stair, ran a fingertip down Ryan's cheek to his jaw, and sighed. "You're only here for the summer. Don't beat yourself up trying to be the man you think I deserve when you're going to leave anyway. Can't we just enjoy each other's company and, I don't know, leave each other better than we found each other?"

"I don't have much luck at leaving people better than I found them."

"My ex-husband is in jail for trying to kill me." The words slipped out. Trey hadn't meant to say them. Hadn't known he *could* say them. The world seemed to slip sideways as he caught his breath, and Ryan's hands were on him, holding him up. That warmth on his skin brought him back to the surface instead of letting him drown in his own shock.

"I don't know what to say," Ryan whispered.

"You don't have to say anything. I just didn't want you to think I had impossibly high standards or anything." Trey's nose stung, and he couldn't meet Ryan's gaze. "I think you're beautiful. And talented. And kind. And I really fucking like you too."

Ryan's arms came around him, and they hugged each other for a long, hard minute, chests heaving. It was Ryan who broke the silence and stepped back.

"I don't have a lot of guy friends. In LA, it was always me and Ali against the world. There's West but . . . there wouldn't even be him if it wasn't for Ali. I don't know how to do this. Do I still get to have hot FaceTime sex with you if we're friends?"

Trey laughed and wiped his eyes on his shoulder. "I don't know, I kind of ruined that with my dumbass comment about your reputation. Maybe we should try doughnuts and getting to know each other next so I don't fuck up on stuff."

Ryan's hands rubbed Trey's arms, grounding him while his mind leaped around for something to cling to other than the confession he'd just made.

"You're shaking; come here, sit down."

They huddled together on the narrow balcony, shoulder to shoulder and knee to knee, with Ryan's arm slung around Trey's shoulders. For a long time they didn't say anything, then Ryan laughed his low cackle, and Trey glanced over at him.

"What?"

"I bet you built epic blanket forts as a kid."

Trey laughed. "Yeah. I always liked building things, and my sisters had bunk beds, which were fucking awesome for blanket-fort building."

"You're gonna be okay." It sounded more like a question than a statement.

"Some days I don't think so. But right now it feels like maybe I am."

"Good."

"Why don't you have a lot of friends? You're good at this stuff."

Shaking his head, Ryan gave him a rueful smile. "I have lots of acquaintances. People who can score me weed on a moment's notice. People who can tell me where to be seen on any given Friday night in WeHo. People who want to sleep with me—or with Ali and figure I'm a good way to get to her."

"People who *use* you."

"I'm a useful guy."

The bitterness in Ryan's voice soured Trey's stomach. "Don't say shit like that. You're a *good* guy. You're smart and funny and hugely talented. You deserve to be around people who want to be around you for those reasons."

"I'm not that smart." Ryan bounced his shoulder against Trey's. "No arguments about my 'talent' though. I've seen enough to know mine is bigger than average."

Trey snorted. "I take back the bit where I said you were funny. Learn to take a compliment."

"Sorry. Thanks."

"You're welcome." Trey ran a finger along the paint at the top of the stairs. "It's just about dry. You need a ride home?"

Ryan shook his head and stood up. "I took West's Volvo. Thanks for letting me help out today. After being a fuckup for years, it's good to be useful. I mean—"

"I know what you meant. And I appreciate the help. It went a lot faster with another set of hands."

"My hands are at your service whenever you want them." Ryan grinned over his shoulder as he descended the stairs.

"I'll keep that in mind."

"Later, Trey."

"Later."

Trey double-checked that the back door was locked and the lights were off in the office, then he dragged the ghost light onto the stage and switched it on.

"You're gonna be okay."

Ryan's words echoed through Trey's head as he turned off the house lights and locked the theater. Maybe Ryan was only here for the summer, but that didn't mean they couldn't be good for each other while it lasted.

Chapter Nine

Trey was pretty damned sure Doc Wharton had moved the seashells around on the waiting room walls in the two weeks since he'd last seen her. Was that even fair? Wasn't she supposed to be a calming, steady influence? Surely she had patients who needed things to stay constant, right?

"Hello, Trey," she called from the door to the hallway. "Why are you scowling at my painting?"

"Did you move those shells around?" He gestured at them as he stood to follow her to her office.

"I did."

Huh. He didn't know what to say to her matter-of-fact answer.

"You don't usually notice things like that." She shut the door behind him and sat down at her desk. "And you missed your appointment last week. How have you been?"

He shrugged. "I almost had a panic attack. I got to the Xanax before it got too bad. But it was weird what triggered it."

"Where were you when this happened?"

"I was at a party on the beach. And Ryan—that's the guy I told you about last time—Ryan reached out like he was going to help me stand up, and it just hit me all at once."

"What happened next?"

"I took a Xanax; he drove me home. We, um—" He blushed and looked at his fingernails. "We made out a little, and then I started getting sleepy, so he went home."

"Let's go back to before you took the Xanax. What happened between Ryan reaching for you and you taking the Xanax? How much time passed?"

What had happened? "I did the naming things trick. I don't know, a few minutes?"

"Good. Did it help?"

"Yeah. I think so."

"It sounds like you handled the attack just like we talked about, and you got through it okay. I'm proud of you."

Relief fizzed along his skin, and he smiled. "Thanks."

"So you saw Ryan again? I'm guessing he's not a tourist?"

Trey shook his head. "No, as a matter of fact, he's an actor."

Her eyebrow shot up. "Shakespeare by the Sea?"

"Yup. But, also TV and movies and stuff. His stage name is Bryan Hart."

"Bryan Hart? *The* Bryan Hart, from *Gravity Wells*? I love that show! What's he doing in Banker's Shoals?"

"Caroline Hertzog is his cousin."

"Huh. Who knew? I can see the resemblance now that you say that." She typed something into her computer. "So, he's here for the summer and you guys are seeing each other? How is that going?"

"I think we're more just friends who make out sometimes."

She paused for a moment, and he wasn't sure, but he thought she might be blushing.

"Okay. How's that going?"

He laughed and ran a hand through his hair. "I told him about my ex."

That made her look up suddenly. "Did you?"

He nodded. "I actually said it out loud. I said, 'My ex-husband is in jail for trying to kill me.' And I thought I was going to fall over, but I didn't. And I just said it again to you, and it was even easier."

"Trey, that's *huge*."

"Yeah." His face flushed at her enthusiasm.

"You should be proud of yourself. This is a legitimate breakthrough! How do you feel about it?"

"Well, he didn't freak out."

She sat back in her chair, smiling. "That's not what I asked."

"I feel good? I'm glad I told him. Luckily I was too surprised to be embarrassed."

"Okay, talk to me about that. Why would you be embarrassed?"

"Because I married a guy who beat the shit out of me. I married him, and I stayed married to him. His shit is still in my garage."

"You aren't to blame for his actions, Trey, he is."

"I know." A spike of anger lanced through him, but faded as quickly as it came. "I don't blame myself, but that doesn't make it any easier to understand how—" He shook his head. They'd talked about this so many times, and every time he was helplessly ashamed for reasons he couldn't articulate and helplessly angry at her for making him examine all the ugly feelings he didn't want to think about.

"Let's leave that for now." She surprised him by giving him a broad smile. "Why do you think you told Ryan?"

He shrugged. "I don't know, actually."

"You've been spending time with him at the theater, seeing him romantically—even inviting him into your home. Obviously you enjoy his company—that's a good foundation for building trust."

Trey nodded. He did trust Ryan. Maybe after his history, trusting someone he'd only recently met was foolish. But Ryan sparked lots of feelings in him that weren't necessarily wise.

"He makes me want to trust him. He's so . . . nice, but also lost, if that makes sense?"

"What do you mean by 'lost'?"

"He's successful enough at his job that people have heard of him, right? But he's here doing summer stock because of some big scandals in the tabloids. He calls himself a fuckup, but from what he's said, most of the things he's done are pretty harmless. I get the feeling he's kind of . . . impulsive? Yeah. Impulsive. But that's part of what's appealing." He paused—it wasn't just Ryan's impulsiveness that was appealing, but the reckless abandon that came with it was enthralling. "And he's fucking sexy."

She laughed. "He sounds like a guy still figuring life out."

"Yeah. I mean, I think he's closer than he realizes. He's amazing."

Ryan found Mason in his office, scowling at his laptop, at six o'clock on Tuesday morning. He'd said good-bye to West, who was flying back to California later, and come to the theater early, forgoing his morning run, because he and Mason needed to have it out once and for all.

He knocked on the doorframe. "Got a minute?"

Mason looked up, scowl deepening. "Yeah, what's up?"

"You and I need to talk. Mind if I shut the door?"

Mason waved at it. He shut the door and sat down. He didn't like upsetting Mason. He'd idolized this man for over a decade. *"You crave approval but settle for attention."* He took a deep breath.

"I'm sorry, Mason, but who I date, or fuck, or whatever, is my business, not yours. I know I promised I wouldn't sleep with anyone in the cast or crew, but the fact is, Trey and I are both consenting adults, and you don't get to tell us we can't see each other."

Leaning back in his chair, Mason stared at him. "I don't?"

"No, you don't."

Mason smiled and shrugged. "Okay."

Ryan stared at him in disbelief. "That's it? Just 'Okay'? What the fuck, Mason?"

"Yeah . . . okay. You're consenting adults. Whatever you want to do."

"So you're telling me you're making a complete one-eighty on what you said before, just like that?"

Mason closed his laptop. "Yes, Ryan. Because you aren't asking my permission. And you don't need my permission. You're not only an adult, you're behaving like one. So, okay."

"Did Caro say something to you?" Ryan squinted, not quite believing what he was hearing. Or, oh god—"Or Trey?"

Mason sighed heavily. "Oh for fuck's sake, Ry. No. You stomp around my theater like a child for a decade, then yeah, I'm going to treat you like one. Two weeks ago, you were still acting like a child. Hell, you're acting like one *now*."

That brought Ryan up short. "All right, well, as long as we agree that you don't get to dictate my sex life." He stood and held out his hand.

With a bemused expression, Mason stood up, clasped his hand, and Ryan led him through an elaborate bro-shake.

"We shook on it; you can't take it back," Ryan warned.

"The only thing I'm taking back is when I said you were behaving like an adult. I'm going to have a smoke, and no, you can't have one."

Ryan followed Mason out to the parking lot and watched him light up. He didn't really understand what had just happened in Mason's office. And he wasn't entirely sure Caro had nothing to do with it.

"Why are you here so early?" he asked.

"Financials. I have to keep the bills paid, not just direct your pretty ass."

"I know that. I guess I didn't realize you came in before sunrise to work on them."

"Speaking of work. I want you to work with Annsley on the party scene—the bit where she turns you down. It's an important moment, and she's playing it for laughs. Which is fine—"

"But she's missing the nuance." Ryan had noticed the same thing. "It's funnier if she nails the poignancy of that moment too."

"Exactly. She's good, but she doesn't have a natural ear for the timing; she hams it up too much."

"I'll work with her."

"Good, take her somewhere this afternoon and work on that scene until she gets it right. And show her how to use her body language better. She moves like she's competing in a beauty pageant."

Ryan flinched. Annsley was stiff, but they'd only been rehearsing for a little over a week. "You cast her."

"Yeah. And I see what she's capable of. Go get it out of her."

So he did.

That afternoon, he took the bubbly, dark-skinned lead actress for a walk on the beach outside the theater. Annsley was vivacious and funny—in some ways, she reminded him of Ali. Her sense of humor, however, tended much more toward the obvious joke, not the sly teasing that had made Ali a reality-TV favorite. He had seen her clowning around with the rest of the cast, but when they were alone together, Annsley usually clammed up. How could he get her to loosen up around him?

They cut through the theater parking lot to the boardwalk, and Ryan stopped to get a pair of sunglasses out of the Volvo. A red Toyota was parked so close, he barely had room to open the door enough to grab them.

"Damn." Annsley shook her head. "People need remedial parking lessons."

"Right?" Ryan locked the car. "I hope he's gone when I get back or I'm gonna have to crawl through the passenger side."

As they stepped off the boardwalk onto the wet sand at low tide, he kicked off his shoes and held his arms out wide. "It's hard to believe in three weeks this place will be crawling with tourists; right now it's paradise."

Annsley laughed and kicked off her own shoes. "Working here is definitely a perk of the job."

"So, Mason asked me to run through the party scene with you. He thinks we're playing it too hard for the laugh."

"You mean *I'm* playing it too hard for the laugh. But thanks for trying to spare my feelings."

"It's a joint effort. Want to run lines?"

"Here?" She gestured toward the waves.

"It's perfect; no one can hear us. And don't try to project now. Try to live in the character for a bit, okay? Start from 'your father.'"

"Um. Okay." She cleared her throat. "Your father got excellent husbands, if a maid could come by them."

He cupped her jaw in his hand. Leaning close, he ran a thumb down the side of her face, as though this were a real proposal, and not a rehearsal for a play. As his thumb slipped over her lips, he murmured, "Will you have me, lady?"

She sucked in a breath, her eyes going wide and her body freezing like a deer in headlights. The breath rushed out of her, then she squared off her shoulders and gave him a sad smile. Taking his hand from her face, she gave it a gentle squeeze and cocked her head to one side.

"No, my lord, unless I might have another for working-days: your grace is too costly to wear every day. But, I beseech your grace, pardon me: I was born to speak all mirth and no matter."

Grinning, Ryan stepped away from her and let out a whoop.

"There. That was perfect. Your body language just there—the way you froze for a moment and then you found yourself? That little hesitation is the nuance that was missing. Can you do that on stage?"

Annsley laughed and turned away, crossing her arms over her chest. "Is that what it would be like for Beatrice when the prince courts her? Like having a celebrity touch her like that?"

Ryan shrugged. "I imagine yes? I don't know. He was a *prince.*"

"So are you, dude." She punched him in the abs, softly though. "I don't know how to play it cool when there's a guy standing in front of me, someone I idolize, who's living my dream, and he's all smooth and—"

"Stop." He grabbed her hands. "First, I'm just a dude. A dude who grew up here on Banker's Shoals. You're probably from some place way cooler."

"I'm from Asheville." She pulled her hands away from him and crossed them over her chest again.

"Well. At least Buncombe is a blue county, am I right?"

She laughed. "Okay, so you grew up here and you made it big, so anyone else can do the same, as long as they wish really hard? Your privilege is showing."

"We both know it's more complicated than that. But you're gorgeous on that stage, and when you deliver the lines like you're feeling them in your soul? It wrecks me. You can do this. You think Mason casts people who can't do the work? That man is the finest Shakespearean actor I've ever seen. He believes in you. I believe in you."

"He cast me as the *lead.*"

"Yes."

"You got a secondary part—I would have cast you as Benedick."

"I'm happy to play Don Pedro—I love this role."

"I thought maybe I'd be lucky to be Ursula or Margaret."

Ah, so that's what's bothering her. Ryan understood this—he'd always been a character actor, never a leading man. Even when his name was the biggest, most well-known in a film, he was always playing somebody's brother or roommate. But if he were in the lead role . . . Yeah, he could definitely see where her brain was tripping up on this.

"Excuse me? Are you Bryan Hart?" A young woman approached them, grinning.

"Um, yeah." He gave Ann an apologetic shrug.

"I can't believe it! Can you sign this for me?" The woman held out a T-shirt. "Hold on, I think I have a Sharpie somewhere—here!" She pulled one out of her beach bag. "This used to be my diaper bag and I wrote the dates on bags of milk after pumping. Thank god for small, strange favors, right?"

"Right. Um, your name?"

"Lorie. L-O-R-I-E. I know, it's weird. I think my mom smoked a lot of pot in the seventies."

Ryan gave her a tight smile, scribbled off a quick inscription— *Dear Lorie, thanks for the luv, Bryan Hart*—and then handed her the Banker's Shoals lighthouse T-shirt back with a grin. "Thanks for watching!" he called after her as she walked away.

"Are you supposed to be doing that?" Annsley asked.

"Doing what?"

"We signed an NDA, dude. Your castmates aren't allowed to acknowledge you're here, and you're signing autographs."

Oh. Oh shit. "Well, I think pretending not to be myself would be a way bigger story than signing an autograph for a random person on the beach, yeah? I mean, who's she going to tell? She isn't press."

Annsley wasn't impressed—and on top of that, she seemed deflated. "Okay, whatever. Let's get back to rehearsing."

"Wait, no. We were talking. This is important. You're nervous about playing the lead?"

"Wouldn't you be? This is my first professional job."

He nodded. "Sure. A working actor getting paid is a glorious thing no matter what role, right? But you got the lead. And now you gotta show them all you've got or you might peak at— What are you, twenty-one?"

"Twenty-two."

"Twenty-two. So, it's more than a paycheck; it's like an audition all over again. That's what scares you?"

She nodded. "Yeah."

"I get that. But what you did just now—we ran through the lines *one* time and you nailed it. You nailed it. What's it going to take to get you to play it like that on stage?"

"I don't know."

"Well, let's do it again until it feels natural. And we can run some other scenes if you like too?"

"You're asking me?" She shrugged. "Sure? I mean—I can use all the help I can get."

"Annsley, you're the star of this production. You deserve to be here. You earned this role."

"Okay." She nodded and smiled, visibly buoyed by the pep talk. "Okay. I deserve to be here. I earned this."

"You really did." He grinned back. "Now, ready to do the work?"

"Yes. Let's do it."

"All right. From 'Your father.'"

Chapter Ten

Who Is the Mystery Girl Spotted Canoodling on the Beach with Bryan Hart?

Oops. Ryan stared at the image under the headline on his phone. It would have made a damned good publicity still if he and Annsley had been acting in a movie. It was tender, intimate—they *did* look like lovers. He skimmed the article—it speculated about how long he may have been seeing the recent UNC graduate. It was actually a nice profile of Ann. The commentary about their cozy embrace on the beach approached saccharine, but not mean-spirited. It was, of course, complete fucking bullshit too. What was Mason going to say? He couldn't really be pissed, could he? Ryan and Annsley had been *rehearsing*. It was ten till six in the morning—Mason would probably be up. If Ryan didn't lace up his running shoes and get out to the beach in the next few minutes, he'd miss his window to see Trey and the beast.

Fuck. He had to deal with this first. He hit the sharing link and texted it to Mason. *Do you want to warn Annsley or should I?*

Mason's reply came a few minutes later, as Ryan was tying his shoes and getting ready to head out the door. *I'm not doing your dirty work, damn it. Clean your own mess.*

About what he'd expected. Oh well. He shoved his phone into the armband, locked up the house, and headed down to the beach.

Ferdinand saw him first, letting out a bark that would have terrified Ryan a few weeks ago. It still gave him pause, even more so when Trey waved and very deliberately unclipped the leash.

Ferdinand's rolls of loose skin flopped and swung as he ran toward Ryan, and the effect was too hilarious to be scary. Ryan braced for impact, only to have the dog stop short and crouch into what could only be described as a bow. Then he abruptly turned and ran back to Trey. Laughing, Ryan followed.

"What's he doing?"

"He wants you to play," Trey called, bending over to pick up a piece of driftwood. When Ferdy got close, Trey threw the driftwood down the beach for Ferdy to chase.

"Hi," he said as Ryan approached. God, he was gorgeous. Ryan hadn't been able to stop thinking about him since the morning they painted the set. The smell of paint and visions of Trey's big, strong body had haunted his dreams—sleeping and waking.

"Hi." Ryan clasped his hands behind his back so he wouldn't reach for Trey. He hadn't seen his photographer-shadow yet this morning, but then, he hadn't seen him when he'd been rehearsing with Annsley, either.

"Did you see—"

"Are you going—"

They laughed.

"You go first," Trey said.

"Did you see the *Herald* this morning?"

Trey squinted at the horizon. "Yeah."

"You know it's not true, right? We were acting—rehearsing a scene."

"Fine." Trey shrugged. "But even if you weren't, even if it were true, it's not like I have any claim."

Ryan stared at him. "Of course you do."

Trey stared back, then shook his head. "Let's walk."

"Trey, come on. You have— *We've* had sex." And why did Ryan want that to mean so much more than Trey seemed to think it did?

"So what? I don't own my lovers. I don't get to make decisions for them. You made it pretty clear the other day you wanted to be friends—and that's fine. Friends is good."

"Okay, that's not what I meant at all. Yes, I want to be friends. But I also want—" He buried his hands in his hair. "Oh my god, why is this so hard when we're sober?"

Trey threw another stick of driftwood for Ferdy, and then put a hand on Ryan's shoulder. "Maybe we shouldn't have this conversation in public."

"What, why not?"

"Because my ideal ending to this talk involves us being naked."

Relief flooded Ryan, and he grinned. "Okay, so, um, so does mine."

Trey bit his lip, almost like he was holding back an answering grin. "You realize any plans we make now are going to feel like just an excuse to get naked together? I've totally ruined our friendship."

"Fuck it. Ruin it, I don't care. Who needs friends anyway?"

A surprised shout of laughter bubbled up out of Trey, and it must have been contagious because Ryan was laughing too, and he couldn't remember the last time he'd felt this light.

"Movie night," he said when he finally stopped laughing long enough to get the words out. "Caro and I do movie night on Thursdays at eight. Why don't you come over and watch with us? And then when she leaves, you stay."

"What about Ferdy?"

Ryan shrugged. "Bring him."

Ryan didn't think anything could dampen his mood, but then he walked into the theater for the *Julius Caesar* rehearsal and everyone glared at him. He glanced down at the phone in his hand. Was he late? No. So why was everyone acting like he'd burst in on them not only late but naked too? He searched out the few friends he'd made in the room, his eyes settling on David. He did that *c'mon man, help me out here* thing with his eyes, hoping David would catch his meaning.

But David glowered, then looked away, clearly furious. It wasn't until David turned his back and knelt down that Ryan saw Annsley. Her hands were shaking and she was crying.

"Ann—" Her name caught in his throat.

He watched helplessly as David handed her a tissue and squeezed her hand, then stood and crossed the stage. Ryan was already stepping backward when David stormed down the aisle to forcefully turn him around and shove him toward the door.

"Outside," David murmured. "She doesn't need to see this."

A frisson of fear slithered icy cold down Ryan's spine. "Dude, I'm not going to fight you."

David raised one eyebrow. "I'm not interested in kicking your ass. I'm not Annsley's daddy, I'm her roommate."

"What happened? It was just a stupid gossipy article written by a hack. It's not that big a deal."

When the heavy front door of the theater had swung shut behind them, David turned to face him. "We were all laughing at it this morning. It *wasn't* a big deal. Then Annsley got on Twitter and checked out your mentions."

"My Twitter men— Oh." Ryan didn't do Twitter much. He liked Instagram better. And he never, ever looked at his mentions.

"Yeah. Most of them are nice, actually—people really happy for you and your new 'girlfriend.' But there's a lot of racist garbage in there too. And that's what's going to come up when you google her name from now on."

Oh god. This was bad. "Shit. I need to talk to her."

"What are you going to say? Leave her alone. You've done enough."

The door opened, and Mason joined them on the steps of the theater, cigarette in hand.

"Well bless your heart," he muttered as he lifted it to his lips to light it. He took a long drag, let out a stream of smoke, and glared at Ryan. "You shit the bed on this one. I cast a fan-fucking-tastic actress and beautiful sister as the lead in this year's comedy, and your so-called 'fans' have her in tears."

"You know, Mason, I can't control what every redneck asshole on the planet says or does. What I can control is how I react to it. I'm going to go talk to her, and fuck you both."

He didn't look over his shoulder to catch their reaction as he made his way back into the theater, and he didn't look at the rest of his castmates when he crossed the stage and approached Annsley. They parted for him, and she stood up.

"I'm sorry, sweetheart," he said. "Are you okay?"

"Damn right, you're sorry." She gave him a small shove and wiped at her eyes, then crossed her arms over her chest. "A little warning would have been nice."

"Those assholes on Twitter are just—well, assholes on Twitter. You're an amazing actress and a beautiful woman, and if that story happened to be true, I'd consider myself a lucky man."

"You always say the nicest things." Her voice dripped sarcasm. Damn, she was making this harder than he expected. Time to try for comic relief.

"Unlike the assholes on Twitter, who you should never, ever listen to."

Rolling her eyes, she shook her head. "It's not like I've never been called names before. Though the sheer volume of it was awful."

He glanced around the theater—the other actors were watching them: some seemed sympathetic, but a lot of them looked angry. None of them would hold his gaze when he met their eyes. The unfairness of it hit him hard. They didn't know what it was like, the dance he had to do with the paparazzi. They didn't— *Oh.*

"I should have told you the paparazzi had been following me. I didn't think. I'm sorry."

"Finally," someone whispered behind them.

Annsley's head snapped up and she glared over Ryan's shoulder at whoever had spoken until there was a murmured "Sorry," then turned her attention back to Ryan.

"Yes, you should have. I get that you're used to this kind of shit, but I'm not. And I had no choice *but* to deal with it because you took that from me."

"I am truly sorry. Seriously, what can I do?"

"Nothing. What's done is done."

"I'm so, so sorry I put you in this position. And the stuff on Twitter—you never should have had to see that."

She laughed a watery laugh. "God, stop groveling. You suck at it. And I'm never looking at your Twitter mentions again, so."

"Good. I never look at them either. Are we okay?"

She nodded. "Yeah, we're okay."

By the time Mason and David returned to the theater, Annsley's face was dry, even if her eyes were still puffy.

"Are we ready to work?" Mason looked at Ryan, not Annsley.

Ryan nodded.

"Ann?" Mason turned to her. "How about you?"

"Yes, absolutely."

"Excellent. We're going to pick up where we left off yesterday on blocking act three, scene two. I need Brutus, Cassius, and the citizens with lines on stage. If you're in the crowd but not speaking, stay seated for now."

Annsley was playing the third citizen, so she squeezed Ryan's hand one last time, and made her way to the stage.

After rehearsal, Mason stopped Ryan outside the theater. As he lit his customary cigarette, he studied Ryan's face. "Thank you for handling that gracefully."

"She's a good kid. I wish I'd understood sooner the position I put her in."

"I don't mean to be an asshole to you."

Ryan's jaw dropped open at Mason's unexpected candor. "Then don't be? I'm trying, dude. I know I fuck up all the time—and you're right to hold me accountable—but I would never have purposefully done anything to hurt Ann, or the theater."

"My temper is short for—" Mason blew out a breath and rubbed his eyes "—for a lot of reasons I can't discuss. But I shouldn't take it out on you, and I'm sorry."

"Apology accepted." Ryan leaned against the wall. "I wish—" He paused. How could he explain to Mason how much his good will meant? "I understand why you don't trust me. But I hope by the time I go back to California, you will."

"It's not that I don't trust you. I cast you, didn't I?" Mason gestured at the theater. "I haven't—I haven't been fair or given you credit for how far you've come. And no, Caro didn't make me say that. When a man does wrong, he admits it."

Ryan warmed at the unfamiliar furrow in Mason's contrite brow. He'd known Mason for a long time. He'd found him by turns intimidating and inspiring, prickly or impassioned, but had never seen him anything less than self-assured. Maybe his expectations of Mason had been every bit as rigid as Mason's expectations of him.

"You gave me a job and a place to figure my shit out. I'm not going to fuck this up. I swear, Mason. This means the world to me—I respect what you do here."

"I know you do." Mason's smile was the most hesitant Ryan had ever seen from him.

"Yeah, we're good." Ryan held out his hand, and Mason shook it, then pulled him into a tentative hug. Ryan clapped Mason's back and grinned. Something major had just shifted in his friendship with Mason—for the first time in many years, they were family again.

Chapter Eleven

Anticipation bubbled and churned in Trey like a glass of champagne as he pressed the Call button on the gate at Ryan's place. Or rather—Ryan's friend's place. It was set back from the main road and a painted wrought iron fence surrounded the property. Ryan buzzed him in, and he drove along a sandy path to a sprawling beach house with a massive front porch and sloping gables. The carpenter in him was immediately covetous. The quality of the craftsmanship shone out from all the small details—the geometric trim on the porch, the stained-glass transoms over the door and windows, the patinated copper weathervane. The house didn't just occupy the landscape, but inhabited it. Its unpretentious charm felt perfect for who Ryan might become ten or twenty years from now, and Trey had a strange yearning to know the friend who so generously allowed him to stay here. Surely Ryan couldn't be the fuckup he believed himself to be if his friends trusted him with this quiet luxury?

All this was on his mind when Ryan threw open the door and grinned at him, but it disappeared when Ryan murmured, "Hi," grabbed his face between both hands, and kissed him deeply. Trey had only a moment to register the sleek slide of tongue slipping into his mouth, before his hands were in Ryan's hair and he had backed him up against a wall. He dropped Ferdy's leash and pushed the door shut with his foot. Time seemed to slow as he tasted the man he'd been thinking of nonstop the last few weeks. A sharp, tense heat flared between them, and Ryan's teeth closed down on his lip. Trey grunted and tugged at Ryan's hair, and they broke the kiss and stared at each other, chests heaving.

"Oh god, I was afraid—" Ryan twisted and squirmed in his grip "—I was afraid this wouldn't be as hot as I remembered."

A laugh rumbled out of Trey's chest, but a bubble of hurt came with it. "Why not? Were you afraid you wouldn't want me sober?"

Ryan's eyes widened, and he grabbed Trey around the waist and pulled them together, chest to chest, groin to groin. Trey's eyes rolled back.

"I want you fucking constantly. I was afraid because I couldn't remember anything about our first night together except being absolutely completely gone for you. And when all you remember is that tug of heat and want and goddamn-I've-got-to-have-him, how do you reconcile that with everything you've had before? My god, Trey. I never wanted anyone the way I want you when I try to remember that drunken night. I wish I could remember it. I really do."

"Why?" Trey rasped, burying his face in the side of Ryan's neck, taking in the sweet smell of his soap and the still-damp scent of his hair. Ryan must have showered before he arrived—maybe even just for him. And the thought of why—not to mention the vision of Ryan's hard movie-star body under a soft spray of water—made him groan. But what Ryan said next floored him.

"Because now that I know you? What kind of man you are? I know we must have been amazing together."

They *had* been amazing, but more amazing was the connection and the trust they'd nurtured since. He pressed his hips into Ryan's and kissed him slow and sweet, drawing it out, nipping at his lips until Ryan let out a husky, wanton gasp and thrust up against him.

"Oh god, Trey, we gotta stop."

Shuddering, Trey pulled his lips away and let his forehead hit the wall with a gentle *thunk*. He wasn't sure if he wanted to growl or whine, and settled for a breathless "Why?"

Ryan laughed and touched Trey's ear, a tender, thoughtless caress. When he followed it with a stroke of his finger along Trey's nose, Trey shuddered. Ryan might not realize he was cataloging the most visible of Trey's old injuries, but Trey felt that touch like a balm he hadn't known he needed.

"Because Caro's gonna be here any minute for movie night. She wouldn't have a problem with us being together, but that doesn't mean she needs a peep show, you know?"

"Oh Christ." Trey pulled back and looked down—both of them were hard, both obviously rumpled. There was no way Caro wouldn't notice immediately what had been going on.

"The powder room is to your right, before you get to the kitchen. I'm going to disappear upstairs for a minute." He glanced down the hallway and smiled. "Ferdy has made himself at home on West's couch—which is fine, but we should put a towel under his face—I'll bring one down with me. Caro will buzz when she gets to the gate; if I'm not back, just hit the button on that panel there that says 'gate' to let her in."

So matter-of-fact. Trey swallowed and nodded, then practically ran to the powder room to straighten himself up. He splashed cold water on his face and thought of unsexy things like doing laundry and cleaning Ferdy's ears. When his hard-on had finally subsided enough that it wasn't tenting his shorts anymore, he combed wet fingers through his hair until it looked halfway normal.

He paused and touched his lumpy, permanently swollen ear with one fingertip. Ryan hadn't prodded him for more information about the beating that had landed him in the hospital and his ex-husband in jail, but he was an observant guy—knowing what he knew, it wouldn't take much for him to put it all together. Maybe he already had.

Trey heard footsteps on the stairs and took a deep breath, then he left the solitude of the powder room. The hallway opened into the living room, and Ferdy was indeed sprawled out on a gigantic couch, all four feet in the air, snoring for all he was worth. Ryan was placing a towel near his head, but didn't wake the dog. He glanced up at Trey and grinned.

"Talk about words I never thought I'd say, but I like your dog."

Trey laughed and reached down to ruffle Ferdy's ears. Ryan caught his hand and pulled him close, giving him a chaste kiss at the corner of his lips.

"Stay."

Trey nodded. "I'm planning on it."

"Good."

Just then, the gate alarm buzzed and Ryan walked away to let Caro in. Trey made himself comfortable on the couch with Ferdy.

A few minutes later, Caro's effusive greetings carried down the hallway, followed by herself, a bundle of energy and wild, sun-streaked curls.

"Trey, hi! Ryan just told me you were here. It's so nice to see you outside of the theater."

"Hey, Caro."

"I brought wine—you guys want a drink?"

Trey shot an inquisitive glance at Ryan, who shook his head slightly. He'd apparently meant what he'd said about not fooling around when they were fucked up.

"I'm not drinking tonight, Carebear," Ryan said quietly. "And I don't think Trey is either. But you can help yourself."

She looked from one to the other, eyes narrowing, then widening. "Okaaay. Well, I'll pass too." Taking a seat on the chair by the window, she folded her legs up underneath her and stared at her cousin.

"So, what's new?" Trey asked, to break the silence.

"I think I've finally talked Mason into selling his place and moving in with me." She grinned.

"What, like roommates?" Ryan sat down next to Trey, who covered his surprise with a cough.

"No, not like roommates," Caro said slowly. "Like partners."

"Why would you move in with your business partner?" Ryan's brows drew together, and he cocked his head to one side.

"He doesn't know?" Trey was incredulous. How could Ryan possibly not know that his cousin and Mason were a couple?

"Doesn't know what?"

Caro shook her head. "Ryan, Mason and I have been together for five years now. You get a joint Christmas card from *us*—not from the theater. From me and Mason. We own a business, yes, but we also . . ." She held up her hands. "How did you not know?"

"But he doesn't—" Ryan stopped. "You don't—"

"That isn't your business," Caro said softly. "I really thought you knew. I'm going to have that glass of wine now." She stood and disappeared into the kitchen, hurt in every line of her body.

Trey could feel the tension in Ryan's body as he turned to face him.

"Really, dude? How did you not know? Haven't you ever *seen* the way they are together?"

"But he's ace," Ryan blurted. "I didn't think . . ."

Trey shook his head. "Like Caro said, that's not your business. They make each other happy, what do you care?"

"I'm just surprised is all. It explains a few things though."

"Yeah, like what? The slow dancing? The fact that they always leave work together? Oh, I know, maybe it's the fact that they finish each other's sentences or that when they're in the same room, they can't take their eyes off each other?"

"More like the fact that Mason is so protective of Caro and sometimes acts like he's my dad or something. God, I'm fucking blind. No wonder he believes I'm self-absorbed."

Trey didn't have anything to say to that. He had spent a lot more time with Caro and Mason over the last five years than Ryan had, and even though neither of them had ever come out and said to him that they were together, and they didn't wear rings, he had thought of them as a unit for so long, he couldn't imagine thinking of them any other way.

Caro walked back into the room, wineglass in hand. "I can't wait to tell Mason about this."

Ryan turned red all the way up to his perfect ears. Adorable. "Please don't."

"Oh, no, I'm gonna tell him. I don't keep secrets from him."

Trey watched in astonishment as Ryan stood and crossed the room with a menacing scowl. Caro shrieked and threw a pillow at her cousin, who snatched the wine from her hand, set it aside, and began tickling her until she was breathless and crying, punching Ryan on the shoulder.

"You fucker." She laughed, wiping her eyes, when he let her go.

"Does he make you happy?"

"Yeah. He really does. And we're going to make it official, get married someday, but we just . . ." She shrugged. "I don't know, that stuff didn't seem important, but lately something's changed. We want that security. I didn't mean to blindside you."

"No, *I* didn't mean to be so self-involved that I was blind to something big and important in your life."

Trey sat still as a stone, watching them with a lump in his throat. If there were an easy way to get Ferdinand and sneak out, he would have, but instead he was a helplessly awkward observer to something that looked an awfully lot like a reconciliation, especially when Ryan whispered in Caro's ear and she started crying and hugging him again. Finally, Trey couldn't stand it anymore. He didn't belong here.

He cleared his throat, and both the Hertzogs turned to him. "I should go," he said, and Ferdy sat up.

"No, don't. I'm sorry, I made everything weird." Caro gave Ryan a little shove, and he came back to sit next to Trey.

"Please stay." Ryan's hand found Trey's thigh and squeezed.

"You know what? Why don't I go?" Caro peered back and forth between them. "I'm not really in the mood for a movie anymore."

Trey started to protest, but Ryan's hand tightened on his leg and he stopped.

"I'll walk you out."

Their low murmurs reached Trey where he sat, but he couldn't make out any words until he heard Ryan shout, "Love you! See you tomorrow!"

He let his head sink against the back of the couch. Ferdy, the traitor, had fallen back to sleep. It seemed his mastiff could sleep through anything except a thunderstorm.

Which left him absolutely nothing but awkwardness.

"Hey." Ryan strolled back into the living room, a wide smile on his face. "So, I'm a big idiot, that's been established. And now things are super weird, and I feel not so sexy. But I found out that I don't get off on humiliation, which is good to know."

Trey couldn't help it, he laughed. Then he stood and crossed over to Ryan. "And here I was the one feeling not so sexy because I was here for this incredibly personal thing that just happened with you and your cousin. I was a total third wheel."

On the couch, Ferdy snorted and twitched.

Trey took Ryan's hand—it was warm and a little damp, like he was as nervous as Trey.

"Do you—do you want to watch a movie?" Ryan whispered, all wide-eyed. He had a dusting of freckles over his nose that Trey hadn't ever noticed before.

"No."

"Neither do I."

Trey's kiss was everything Ryan needed in that moment to set his mind at ease. Gentle, for about half a second, then Ryan's face was clutched in Trey's hands and his lips yielded to rough bites and a demanding tongue. Ryan whimpered and let go of his nerves, clinging to Trey's waist with both hands. "God, yes."

Trey pulled back. "What's in your backyard? A swimming pool?"

Ryan shook his head. Why the hell would Trey want to go swimming? "No, just a hot tub, a few lawn chairs, a hammock. Path down to the beach, but I don't really want to walk on the beach right now."

"Is the hot tub covered?"

"Yeah. Why?"

"Can we leave the door cracked for Ferdy?"

Relieved, Ryan nodded. "Sure. I mean, I don't think West gives a flying fuck about the AC bill." He crossed to the sliding door that led out to the patio and opened it, letting the warm ocean breeze blow into the living room. Then he took Trey's hand and led him upstairs.

The guest room was decorated in wide navy-blue stripes on white, with whitewashed paneling and walnut floors. In the weeks he'd been living here, he'd never thought of it as anything more than a convenient place to sleep, but when he pushed Trey down onto the soft white bed and saw his strawberry-blond stubble glinting in the twilight glowing through the window, he couldn't help but think it was the perfect nautical backdrop for the brawny townie. A million "captured by the pirate" fantasies ricocheted through his head, flushing his face and hardening his dick.

"What are you thinking?" Trey skimmed a finger over his cheekbones. "To make you turn pink like this? Take off your shirt, I want to see how far that blush goes."

Ryan tugged his shirt off and tossed it over his shoulder, then started divesting Trey of his too. "You look like a pirate. I don't know, maybe it's just the room. But it gave me some crazy-dirty thoughts."

Chuckling low and filthy, Trey rolled Ryan until they were both lying on their sides, and he kissed him again.

"I'd kiss you for hours."

Ryan whimpered into Trey's mouth and let himself get carried away by the rhythm of their bodies rolling and thrusting together. Heat rippled between them, sparking higher everywhere their bodies touched, and accelerated by throaty noises and lush kisses.

When Trey's hands skimmed over Ryan's nipples, Ryan arched and whined; when they pinched, he gasped and shuddered.

"God, yeah."

Trey leaned in close, clutching Ryan's chin in one hand, and bit at his Adam's apple, sending a shiver of delight through his whole body.

"Can I take these off?" Trey tugged at the waistband of Ryan's shorts with his other hand, and Ryan shoved at them, as anxious to be naked with Trey as he'd ever been for anything in his whole life.

"Shhh. Slow down." Trey, still holding his face, kissed him again, slowly and thoroughly, tightening his hand slightly when Ryan tried to hurry him along by reaching for his shorts again. Ryan groaned and acquiesced, let Trey ease down his body and strip them away.

"I want you to remember everything this time," Trey whispered, so softly, Ryan wasn't sure he heard it correctly, but then Trey met his gaze and smiled, lips quirking up in a way that had become so familiar, so dear, over the last couple weeks. Ryan reached for the big, beautiful man who was the closest friend he had here on Banker's Shoals.

Trey kissed him again then, teasing, plucking kisses at first, then lush and openmouthed, like he could kiss straight into Ryan's soul—and maybe he could, because Ryan couldn't remember the last time someone had made him feel this good. He arched up his hips, trying to get friction on his cock, and Trey broke the kiss.

"Lie back, I've got you," he murmured, and Ryan sank back against the pillow, hotly aware that Trey still had his pants on, and Ryan was naked as a jay. But then Trey's hand found Ryan's dick, and clothing didn't seem important at all. Ryan let his head drop back and his legs drop open while Trey kissed him, by turns gentle and rough, all the while slowly pumping Ryan's cock.

Pleasure seemed to slide along every nerve ending, and a low moan escaped his lips.

"Do you have lube?" Trey asked quietly, almost against Ryan's lips, and Ryan nodded.

"In the bathroom."

Trey laughed, a soft huff, then guided Ryan's hand to his own dick. "Inconvenient. Here, don't you dare come. But keep yourself . . . happy. Which door?"

Ryan gave his dick a gentle stroke. "Left out my door, first on right."

Trey's warmth disappeared from the bed as he left on his quest, but he returned a moment later, naked and glorious. He was all hard muscle and copper-gold hairs, with a black smudge of tattoo over his hip bone, and everything about him made Ryan ache with want. Trey set a strip of condoms down on the bedside table, and Ryan chuckled.

"Ambitious?"

Trey smiled. "Hopeful."

Snick. A lube bottle opened, and Ryan watched Trey's face as he poured a bit on his fingers and then gave Ryan the wickedest, dirtiest smile he'd ever seen.

Trey's lube-slick hand stroked over Ryan's dick first, making him thrust up eagerly, then it slid lower, caressing his balls, and then lower still, to that spot on his taint that made him cry out. *Holy fuck.*

"You said you like ass play," Trey murmured. "And I want to make you shoot sparks."

Trey massaged his prostate from the outside, then dipped a finger inside like he was just testing the waters. Ryan nearly jerked up off the bed, but Trey's other hand was there, shoving his chest back down, and then his lips were on Ryan's and Ryan's hands were in Trey's hair, and there were *two* fingers probing his ass.

"Unh—damn, Trey," he whined as Trey's thumb nudged the same spot from the outside that his fingers were stroking on the inside.

He felt like he was boiling out of his skin, and his dick was leaking a stream of white fluid. He was going to come, and that wasn't what he wanted—he wanted Trey inside his body, Trey as far gone as he was, Trey biting his *own* lip and shouting.

"No, please." He shoved at Trey's arm. "Both of us. It's got to be both of us."

Trey reared up over him and reached for a condom. He tore the wrapper with his teeth, rolled the rubber over his gorgeous cut dick, and then lined himself up.

"Is this what you want?"

It wasn't a teasing, mocking "tell me you want my dick, bitch" sort of comment—but something else, something quiet and sincere, and Ryan nodded, a smile turning up his lips. "More than anything."

And with that, Trey slipped inside him as gently as possible, but he was big—thick—and Ryan winced a little before Trey's fingers wrapped around his dick and stroked it fully hard again.

Then their lips came back together, and Ryan was gone. "Oh please, please," he murmured into Trey's mouth, hands clutching at broad shoulders as Trey glided in and out in a devastating rhythm. Time seemed to slow as their bodies rocked, and Trey's hands grasped at Ryan's own, entwining their fingers.

The storm building between them was bigger and hotter than anything Ryan had ever known. He'd never *wanted* like this, never *felt* wanted like this, and when Trey bit the side of his jaw, rough and demanding, he arched up and *begged*.

"Please don't stop, please."

Trey let out a low growl and started driving into him harder, wilder. With their hands clasped over his head, Ryan couldn't get any friction on his cock at all, but Trey's dick was punching his prostate, and there was a tightening happening everywhere until he threw his head back and shouted, pleasure releasing like a tightly bound spring set loose.

He arched and shuddered, both pinned and sheltered by Trey's big body as his orgasm wrung every ounce of sensation from him, and he sank back, sore and sated as the fog of pleasure cleared.

Trey eased out of him and tugged the condom off, then lay down next to Ryan. "Are you okay?" he murmured, and Ryan nodded.

"You should—you should finish."

"I will, roll onto your side."

Ryan, practically boneless, did as he was told, pressing his back to Trey's front, then sighed happily as Trey's cock slipped between his legs, thrusting into the hard flesh of his thighs. As much as he could, he tightened those muscles around Trey's dick, and then a shock of wet heat splashed between his legs as Trey's teeth came down on his shoulder and Trey groaned, long and low, before collapsing down to the bed with Ryan.

Ryan, whose muscles had gone lax and whose bones seemed to have disappeared altogether, clumsily reached over his shoulder and tugged Trey's face to his in a sloppy, desperate kiss. When Trey pulled away and left the bed, Ryan whimpered, too strung out to express his protest with words.

"I'm coming right back. I'm gonna get rid of the condom and get something to clean us up." Trey leaned over him and kissed him long and sweet. "Don't go anywhere."

As if he could. Ryan flopped onto his back and threw an arm across his eyes, letting out a contented sigh. He could hear Trey in the bathroom, flushing the toilet, then running water and washing his hands. A moment later, Trey returned and washed their spunk from Ryan's body with a hot washcloth before disappearing again.

When he came back, the lumbering bulk of his dog followed him, then curled up onto the blue braided rug that dominated the floor.

"I locked the doors downstairs," Trey murmured as he wrapped his body around Ryan's and tangled their fingers together.

Ryan sighed and let his head loll back on Trey's shoulder.

"Are you okay?"

"Mmm. Yeah. You fucked me senseless."

Trey's laugh was a filthy rumble. "That was *fun*."

A smile dragged Ryan's lips up. "Yeah, it was."

"Can we do it again?"

"Ask me in the morning."

They didn't make it until morning, though, before Ryan came down Trey's throat as Trey milked his prostate with two fingers, or before Ryan returned the favor. By the time the sun came up, they'd shared so many orgasms, Ryan wasn't sure how he'd be able to stand at rehearsal in a few hours, but he didn't care. A sore ass and wobbly knees were a small price to pay for the kind of night they'd shared, and they were a price he'd gladly pay over and over again. Whatever would happen at the end of the summer, he had these moments with Trey, and he intended to enjoy them to the fullest.

Trey sat up suddenly in an unfamiliar bed, alone, but surrounded by the scent of sex. He could hear a shower running nearby, and Ferdy was curled at the foot of the bed. *Ryan*.

The images of Ryan that spun through his head had his dick hardening and his sore body screaming to life. God, what a night. When was the last time he'd had epic sex? Ever? Ryan hadn't been kidding about how much he enjoyed ass play, and that was something Trey hadn't gotten to indulge in with a partner in *years*.

Absently, he stroked his cock. He'd be jerking off for years to the memory of Ryan coming hands-free. He'd never seen anything like it, and it made him feel powerful and hot.

"Mmm, save that for me." Ryan appeared in the doorway, smirking, with a towel hanging low on his hips and another wrapped around his hair.

"We don't have time." Trey let go of his dick. "But if you want to take care of it tonight, I'd gladly consider it a date."

Ryan climbed back onto the bed, tossing the towel from his waist aside and straddling Trey. "I can't tonight. The cast is going to the mainland to some stupid oyster bar David and Zach say is amazing. Bonding opportunity. But call me in the morning tomorrow and we'll do something."

Their lips met—tentatively at first, then more confidently as Ryan rolled his cock against Trey's. Reluctantly, Trey broke the kiss.

"Okay. Tomorrow sounds good. Do you get up early on the weekends?"

"No, god. Please, if you love me, let me sleep in."

Trey froze, felt an answering stiffness in Ryan, then relaxed. He didn't mean it like that. He was only here for the summer, and he was being flippant with his words.

"I seem to recall that last time I woke you early, there was filthy FaceTime sex."

"I would wake up for that." Ryan laughed, kissed him one last time, and stood up. "I have rehearsal in an hour. I hate to kick you out, but the alarm system is complicated, and I—"

"Say no more." Trey held up his hands. "I'll get dressed, get Ferdy, and we'll go."

He didn't need much time to get dressed. He hadn't brought an overnight bag—an epic lack of foresight on his part—but he turned his briefs inside out, decided to forgo socks altogether, and borrowed Ryan's deodorant. When his own T-shirt didn't pass the sniff test, he swiped one of Ryan's.

It would have to do.

At the front door, he kissed Ryan deep and slow, until they were both weak in the knees and gasping for breath. Finally, Ferdy shoved his head between the two of them, and they pulled apart, laughing.

"Last night was amazing," Ryan whispered. "And this time, I won't forget it."

Trey smiled and ran his thumb across Ryan's lips. "I plan on reminding you anyway."

"I can't wait."

Chapter Twelve

The phone rang early on Saturday morning. Expecting it to be Trey, Ryan reached for the phone with a smile already on his face, a smile that widened in delight and surprise when Ali's grinning photo appeared on his screen.

"Oh my god, baby, is it really you?"

"Hiya, Rya," she singsonged. "Did you miss me?"

"God, yes. Are you out? Has it been eight weeks already?"

"No, I wish. I'm still here, but I've graduated to phone-use-allowed now that I'm at the six-week mark. Of course, the only person I wanted to call was you."

"I've been dying to hear your voice. I'm so used to talking to you every day, I feel like my right arm has gone missing."

"I know, me too. This has been good for me, though. I'm so much stronger than I was even a week ago."

"It makes me so happy to hear that. I've been worried." He twisted the corner of his sheet around his finger. Should he tell Ali about West's visit? Hell, he never was any good at keeping secrets. "West came out here. It was nice to see him, but I think it just made me miss you more."

"Oh. Was he there about the pilot?" Her voice went all hushed.

"Are you sure you're allowed to have your phone? You're whispering like you stole it."

"Don't dodge. Was he there about our show?"

"He was. How come you didn't tell me you were writing a script?" He tried to keep the accusation out of his voice, but it stung to know that she'd been working on something so huge and had never mentioned it. Wasn't he her best friend too? Didn't she trust him?

"You know how come. I was scared. What if it was a mess that never got sold? What if I was a complete fuckup failure? I didn't want to get my hopes up, and I didn't want to get your hopes up either. You look like a kicked puppy when I flub an audition."

"I do not." A kicked puppy? He was disappointed for her when she didn't get a job she wanted. But he tried to be encouraging.

"Yeah, you do. You seem to care more about my career prospects than your own. So I didn't tell you because if it didn't work out, well. Better if you didn't know."

"How can it be better? Better for who?" Wow, that sounded pretty butt-hurt, didn't it? So much for keeping accusation out of his voice.

"Better for me. I couldn't handle your expectations and worries on top of my own."

"But I could have helped. I could have cheered you on. I—"

"I had West for that, Ry." She sighed heavily. "This wasn't about you. It had literally nothing to do with you. I didn't tell you because it was mine, and I wasn't ready to share, okay?"

Ouch. But what could he say to that? It really *wasn't* about him. "Okay. I'm sorry. I *am* happy for you. I just wish I could have been happy for you sooner."

"You big goober. My keeping this a secret doesn't mean I don't love you, okay?"

"I know."

"So, I need to ask you a huge favor."

Ryan blinked at the sudden change of subject. "Okay."

"I know you're staying at West's beach house. I'm leaving here in two more weeks, and I'm super not ready to go back to LA. Can I come stay with you? And can you maybe not tell West? I need a place to re-acclimate to the outside world."

"You're in rehab, not prison."

"Uh-huh. You dodged my question again."

"Of course you can stay with me, that shouldn't even be a question. But why do you want to keep it a secret from West?"

"Because he's the reason I'm super not ready to return to LA? Please, Ry? I'll explain everything when I get there. No secrets."

"Okay, I won't tell him, but I'm not gonna lie to him either."

"You won't need to, I promise. I would never ask you to do that for me."

Neither one of them pointed out that lying for Ali had once come as easily to Ryan as consoling her when she didn't get a role.

They talked for a few more minutes, mostly about summer stock antics, with Ali laughing along gamely in all the right places, and empathizing when he told her what had happened with Annsley.

"That poor girl. Twitter is awful to women."

He didn't tell her about Trey—and he wasn't sure why. He told her about David hitting on him, and about Caro and Mason's relationship that he'd been too blind to see, but every time he thought he was ready to tell her about Trey, the subject changed, and before long, she said she had to go to a therapy appointment.

Ryan's chest twinged—he hated saying good-bye to Ali. "Now you've got your phone, text me or call me when you can. I'm in rehearsals all day, but I can usually talk in the evenings, okay?"

"Okay. Love you."

"Love you too, baby. See you in two weeks."

Two weeks. Ali was going to be here in two *weeks.* She'd be here for opening night. And she was going to be staying with him in West's house, without saying a word to West.

This was either going to be epic—or an epic disaster.

Trey took Ferdy for a long walk on the beach Saturday morning before he called Ryan. As much as filthy FaceTime sex appealed to him, the idea of waiting until he could get his hands on Ryan in person again appealed so much more. He'd been floating around on a cloud of well-fucked bliss for more than twenty-four hours, and was sex drunk and shivery-spined, with aches in muscles that he'd forgotten how to use.

Like the muscles that made up his smile.

Now, he couldn't seem to shake it off his face. He found himself grinning at strangers, those early tourists catching the last weeks of quiet before the summer hordes descended. A June morning on the ocean still clung to the chill of spring, but by afternoon the sand would shimmer with heat. He and Ferdy lingered until the beach was warm enough that girls in bikinis started sprawling out on bright towels and turning their faces and well-oiled midriffs to the sun.

"C'mon, Peanut. Time to go." He gave a little tug on Ferdy's leash. "Time to call our boy."

When they got back to the house, he reached down to where he usually clipped his key to Ferdy's collar, but it wasn't there.

"Shit. Fuck." He tapped his pockets. *Goddamn it. Okay, don't panic. Don't panic. Where could they be?*

Peering in the sidelight windows, he breathed a deep sigh of relief—they were lying on the kitchen countertop, safely locked inside.

His relief was short-lived though—he was still fucking locked *outside*. With Ferdy, whose tongue was hanging out as he panted in the sun. And the only way into his house was to punch the code on the garage door and cut through.

He could do that. So what if his palms had started sweating? So what if he didn't use the garage, ever? He could do this. He could do it for Ferdy, if not himself.

He pulled his phone out of his pocket and hovered over the first two numbers in his speed dial. Kim and Caro both had spare keys to his place for the rare occasions he needed a Ferdy-sitter. But it would be stupid to call someone to come over when he could just go through the garage.

They would understand.

He tapped the recent calls and found Ryan's smiling face, and before he could think better of it, he called.

"Hey, oh my god, I've got the best news."

He couldn't help himself; he laughed. "It's good to hear your voice too."

"Oh. Shit, I'm sorry. Is this— I mean. Okay. Let's start over. Hey, Trey—oh that rhymes! Okay. Hi, Trey, how are you today? Holy shit, does your name rhyme with everything?"

Trey blew out a breath, looked down at Ferdy, and then ran a hand through his hair. He was a fucking idiot, and he was making an ass out of himself in front of the hottest guy he'd ever met—who just happened to be listing all the words he could think of that rhymed with *Trey*. "Hi, Ryan. Can you chill for a sec? I need . . . I need help. I'm locked out of my house."

"Okay. What can I do? Do you have a spare key somewhere? You should get one of those safe-things."

"I don't need a safe. I just need to know, do you ever get scared, like before an audition or something?"

"Sure. Of course." The giddiness dropped out of Ryan's voice. "What does that have to do with being locked out of your house?"

"It's hard to— Never mind that. Tell me how you work through it."

Silence stretched over the line for a long moment.

"Are you there?" Trey prodded.

"Yeah, um. Well, it sounds silly, but I sing lullabies to myself."

"Lullabies?"

"Yeah. Like 'Hush little baby, don't say a word' and 'Rockabye Baby.' It's stupid, but it works, calms me down."

"Will you sing one for me?"

"Seriously?"

"Fucking-A, Ryan," Trey snapped. "Do you think I'd be asking for this shit if I didn't need it?"

"Sure. Okay. Let's do this." Ryan hummed a few bars of something Trey didn't recognize, then started singing in another language— French maybe? Trey couldn't understand the words, but the melody was soothing and Ryan's voice was nice—a little gravelly in the low parts but sweet and pure when he hit his falsetto.

Trey took a deep breath and punched in the code on his garage door opener.

He kept his eyes shut as the door rolled up, listening to Ryan's voice. Ferdy tugged the leash, moving through the garage to the door. Trey let himself be towed along, sweating like a whore in church, until they were through the door, in the kitchen. He smacked the Door Close button, harder than he needed to, and then shut the door behind him and sank to the floor.

"Thank you."

Ryan laughed, not like he was making fun, more like a sweet rumble of solidarity. "You're welcome. My Cajun uncle—who I don't think was actually related to my dad, but whatever—used to sing that to me."

"Yeah? What's it about?"

"Near as I can tell, something about a white chicken. Which is probably what I looked like as a baby."

Trey chuckled. "Didn't we all? Listen, thank you. I—I can't really explain. I don't know, maybe I can. But it's gonna be the most boring date ever. You want to come over and hang out with me while I clean out my garage?"

Chapter Thirteen

Ryan took the keys to West's Volvo off the hook in the garage, gave the Ferrari a longing look, and sighed. West's affection for sports cars—and the collection of them he'd accumulated—was Hollywood legend. Ryan had promised his agent under no circumstances would he drive the flashy red supercar around the island. It attracted too much attention, and he was supposed to be lying low. It was one thing to ride along the coast with West—another to park it outside Trey's house.

Where he was going to find out more about Trey, in a "this is deeper than a summer fling" way. And is that even what he wanted? To get in that deep with this guy? He was the one who'd said he wanted a friend. Damn. He couldn't just not be a friend back—no matter how much it would suck to leave at the end of the summer, he was in it now, and he'd see it through.

When he pulled into Trey's driveway, the man himself was sitting on the front steps, holding Ferdy's leash.

"Are you still locked out?" he called.

"Nah. We were just waiting for you out here so this big drooly bastard wouldn't knock things over saying hello. I think he likes you." Trey smiled at him and let Ferdy off the leash. Ryan braced himself for impact, and sure enough, the dog came straight for his balls, then sniffed down his legs and back up, spreading drool the whole way.

"Hi, Ferdy." Ryan petted the top of the dog's head gently. "How's it going, big guy?"

He walked past the dog to Trey, gave a quick peek over his shoulder to make sure he hadn't been followed, and gave Trey's hand a squeeze. "Should we go inside?"

"Yeah. Um, before we—c'mon Ferdy—before we go out to the garage, I need to explain a few things."

"Okay."

They sat on Trey's giant sectional, and Ferdy returned to his mattress, rolled onto his back, and fell asleep with all four feet in the air.

"So, I bought this house with Vincent, my ex— Are you comfortable?"

"Yeah, man. Are you?"

Trey shook his head and stood up. "We bought this place when we first moved here, and um, we lived here together for a few years."

"It's a nice place," Ryan offered.

"Thanks." Trey ran a hand through his hair, and Ryan's heart went out to him. He was obviously working up to tell his story, and his nerves were getting in the way.

"Come here." Ryan patted the couch next to him. "Come sit with me."

Trey did as he was told, almost absently. When he sat down, Ryan turned them both so Trey was lying on Ryan's chest, between his legs. He wrapped both arms around Trey and squeezed. The skin of Trey's back was damp through his T-shirt, and his breathing was rushed and shallow, but as he snuggled against Ryan, it began to even out.

"Now, tell me about the garage."

"That was where he went to get away from me. It was his mancave. Mine was the theater."

Ryan nodded. "Okay."

"Vincent was . . . abusive. When he got angry—which was a lot—he would yell, throw things. He would hit things. The walls, doors, anything that got in his way—and me. If I defended myself, if I hit back, I felt bad, and I ended up apologizing. Eventually, I stopped going in the garage because that's where we had so many fights."

"And he's in jail now? Does he still own part of the house?"

"Yes. And no. I bought him out as part of the divorce settlement."

"Okay."

In a flat, quiet voice, as if he were reciting something by rote, Trey continued. "One night I came home from the theater and he was in a mood. Violent. Angry. Throwing things in the kitchen. He beat the shit out of me—broke my nose and cracked two ribs, then stabbed me with a boning knife, and left me bleeding on the kitchen floor."

"Jesus." Ryan shuddered and held Trey closer. The deadpan, emotionless way Trey was describing what had happened chilled him to the bone.

"If we'd owned a gun, I'd be dead. I have no doubt of that. Anyway, I had left my phone at the theater. Caro brought it over and found me half-dead. She managed to do basic first aid *and* keep me conscious until the ambulance got there. She saved my life. And after she made her report to the police, she got me a divorce lawyer."

Ryan's hand clutched over Trey's heart—how close had he come to never meeting this beautiful man? The thought made him dizzy and helpless. "I can't believe anyone would want to hurt you."

"Vincent wanted to hurt the world. Rage and entitlement were a big black hole in his life, sucking everything happy into it. Including me. I think he was always like that—but when we first met, he was really sweet to me. And he was good-looking. Charm plus looks are a potent combo." Trey sighed and snuggled closer to Ryan's chest. "But . . . the signs were there. I just didn't want to see them, and he made me feel like maybe the situation wasn't how it seemed. He didn't remember things happening the same way I did—sometimes he didn't remember them happening at all. So many times I felt like I was losing my mind."

"He was gas-lighting you."

"Yeah. I didn't know the word back then. Boy, do I know it now."

"So the garage? You don't go out there because it's a trigger for your anxiety?"

"Yeah. I don't even know what's out there. I don't want any of it. Legally I own everything in the house, but I don't give a fuck. I don't want anything he's touched."

"All right." Ryan nodded. "How long has it been?"

"A year and a half. My therapist thinks it would be good for me to reclaim that space, but every time I try, I have a panic attack."

Ryan ran a finger down the side of Trey's neck, absently tracing the cords of working-man muscle. "Why don't we call someone to come remove it, then?"

"What?" Trey looked over his shoulder at Ryan. "What do you mean?"

"We call someone to come clean out the garage. They sell anything of value and cut you a check, minus their fees. They dispose of everything else. You don't have to look at any of it, you don't have to deal with it, and your garage becomes yours again."

"This is a thing people do?" Trey's voice was incredulous.

"What do you think happens when someone dies if they don't have family? Or if their family doesn't want to deal with their shit?"

"But no one died," Trey pointed out.

"So what? That doesn't mean the people who provide those services wouldn't take the job. I doubt they care whose shit they're clearing out and selling off, as long as they get their cut."

"I don't know if I can afford it—what if they don't make enough from selling off the stuff to cover their fees?"

"How about you let me handle that?"

Trey began to protest, as Ryan had known he would.

Ryan held up a hand. "Please consider it a gift from a friend. It doesn't mean you owe me anything. And I've got plenty of money. My agent and manager made sure I didn't shove it all up my nose."

"But—"

"Let me help. Please?"

Trey sighed and rolled over, pressing their chests together. He studied Ryan's face for a long time, long enough that Ryan started to get nervous, but then Trey smiled, and his lips found Ryan's, and they were kissing like it was breathing.

"So, that's a yes?" Ryan asked as he pulled away.

"Yes. And thank you. I don't even know how to say all the things floating around in my head. Why would you do this for someone you just met?"

"Okay, first of all, I've been on the island for weeks now, and I met you the same night I got here. Second of all, I like you. A lot. This is something I can do for you, and it will make me feel good to be there. It means something—taking care of each other. That's what friends do."

"I don't think I've ever had a friend quite like you before. Unless we're counting your cousin, but I don't want to kiss her senseless."

Trey kissed him again, this time letting the heat build between them until they were both gasping and grinding together.

"Come on, come back to my bedroom." Trey stood and stretched out his hand.

"I don't—" Ryan shuddered, because yeah, he wanted to. "I don't want you to go to bed with me out of gratitude."

Trey grabbed his hand and yanked him to his feet. "I'm inviting you to my bed because you're sexy and I fucking can't wait to have you fuck me. While I am absolutely grateful for your unexpected insight into my situation, I'd be even more grateful for your dick in my ass right now. Okay?"

Ryan's eye widened, clearly stunned, and it was adorable. How had he lived to be twenty-five years old, in Hollywood, and without hearing that kind of candid dirty talk? Trey was starting to think Ryan was far more sheltered than either of them believed.

"Or if you'd rather I fuck you—I mean, I don't really care one way or the other?"

Ryan opened and closed his mouth like a fish, then honest-to-god blushed to the roots of his hair. "You're so— Gah, I don't have words for what you are. Take me to your bedroom? Last time I left my briefs on your living room floor, Ferdy had them for breakfast."

Laughter bubbled up out of Trey, and he kissed Ryan again, backing him up against the wall as they moved toward the bedroom. He ran his hands down Ryan's hard chest, then up under his shirt, scraping his nails over hot skin, and Ryan squirmed and made a delicious pleading whimper, breaking the kiss and turning his head to the side. Trey dove in. There was a spot behind Ryan's ear that always ramped him up—*there*. Nothing was hotter than the way Ryan responded to a graze of teeth—half laugh, half whine, breathless and impatient and grinding his dick against Trey's leg.

They stumbled into the bedroom, tugging at clothes and grinning—God, was he ever going to get enough of Ryan's laugh? He yanked Ryan's shirt over his head, threw it on the floor, and got his hands back on Ryan's face, giving in to the urge to plant rough, biting kisses on those gorgeous lips until Ryan let out a low moan and shoved him onto the bed.

They rolled and wrestled, kicking the rest of their clothing away until they were both naked and Trey had Ryan pinned. Ryan's hand came up and stroked Trey's ear, then cradled the side of his face, drawing a shuddery breath from Trey.

Time slowed as he leaned down and indulged himself in another deep kiss—the urgency was still there, he couldn't imagine ever not *craving* Ryan—but somehow, in spite of it, holding on to Ryan and kissing him like their lives depended on it was just as good.

"Will you fuck me?" he finally asked, staring into Ryan's steady hazel gaze.

Ryan bit his lip and looked down their bodies to where their cocks rubbed against each other.

"I've never done it before. I always liked bottoming so much—"

"I love topping you. If you want to do it like we've always done, that's fine. I like bottoming too, though. I can't stop thinking about how good you'd feel inside me."

"You'll tell me if I do something wrong?"

Trey kissed him again, slow and dirty, and nipped his lower lip. "It's you and me together. Nothing about it can be *wrong*. But I'll tell you if anything you do doesn't work for me. It's just sex, love. It's not a performance."

Ryan's low breathy laugh was the only warning Trey got before Ryan rolled them over and reversed their positions. "Okay, then lie back and let me play for a bit." He sat up, straddling Trey's chest and reaching for the stash of condoms and lube in Trey's drawer. They hit the bed with a *thump*, and then Ryan started exploring.

Trey stretched his arms above his head and grabbed the headboard, taking a deep breath and closing his eyes. Ryan's hands slid down his chest as soft as a whisper, teasing nipples and tickling the strawberry-blond hair around Trey's navel. When he took a nipple between his thumb and finger and rolled it gently, pleasure shot through Trey and his hips jerked.

"Mmm." Ryan moved to the other nipple and gave it the same treatment, then he made his way down Trey's body. He paused for a moment over the small tattoo above Trey's hip. "It's a circle?"

Trey shrugged, as best he could while holding on to the headboard. "I wanted to cover the stabbing scar—I didn't care if it was pretty, I just wanted it to be mine."

Brushing his lips over the small black circle, Ryan took Trey's dick in one hand. A long lick, a slow stroke, and Trey was ready to promise him anything he wanted if he'd only hurry up. But hurrying didn't seem to be Ryan's style. He played with Trey's dick, tonguing the head, sucking it, rolling his balls and giving them gentle tugs. Trey couldn't keep his hips still; he rocked upward with every new sensation Ryan gave him.

"Oh god," Trey murmured. "That's good." He lifted his knees and put his feet on the bed, hoping Ryan would take the hint and keep exploring. When one spit-slick finger probed him, he let out a rough sigh and couldn't hold on to the headboard anymore. He buried his hands in Ryan's hair and groaned.

Ryan fumbled around for the lube, looking up at Trey and giving him a sweetly wicked smile, then he applied himself to opening Trey like it was his job. Being the utter focus of Ryan's concentration took Trey's breath away. Nothing made him feel more vulnerable than opening his body to another person, letting them inside and trusting them to make it good.

"Are you comfortable on your back?" Ryan asked.

This is really happening. Trey shuddered, nodded, and drew Ryan to him for a kiss.

Ryan's tongue was still sliding into his mouth when his cock breached Trey's ass. The slick slide and sharp spike of pain made Trey gasp, and Ryan pulled back.

"Okay?"

Trey nodded, letting out a breath and bearing down to take Ryan deep inside.

"You feel amazing." Ryan took up a tentative rhythm, and when Trey rolled his hips into it, Ryan seemed to find his confidence.

Grabbing his dick in one hand, Trey reached for Ryan with the other, and then they were kissing and fucking and everything was perfect— he could have cried. The heat built, fast and sharp and so good Trey wanted to live in that moment forever. Too soon, the orgasm he tried to hold back was set off by a particularly enthusiastic thrust, and he came, crying out into Ryan's mouth.

Ryan kissed him through it, then dropped his hands to Trey's hips and drove into him in that erratic, excited way of a man on the verge of coming, and then it was Trey's turn to hold him through the convulsions of pleasure.

Ryan slumped down on the bed and slowly withdrew from Trey's body. Trey wiped them down with a T-shirt from the floor, tugged the blankets up over them both, and held up the trash can for Ryan. As Ryan disposed of the condom, Trey's eyelids started to drag downward.

"You okay?" Ryan murmured.

"Perfect." He fell asleep like that, there with Ryan's head on his shoulder and arms around his waist.

Chapter Fourteen

Ryan woke in the warm circle of Trey's arms, sticky and sated, as the late-afternoon sunlight winked around the edges of the shades. He looked up and saw Trey's eyes were open, and he was smiling.

"Didn't want to wake you," Trey whispered as Ryan stretched to kiss him.

Would he ever get over the softness of Trey's lips against his, the intensity of kissing like this? "God, you slay me. Can we just stay in bed for the rest of our lives?"

"We need to get up to eat and pee and let Ferdy eat and pee, but other than that I am firmly on board with that plan."

As if in agreement, Ryan's stomach rumbled. Trey laughed, ran a warm hand over Ryan's abs, and kissed him again. "I think I can scrounge something up to cook, if you're hungry?"

"Sure. You cook?"

Trey shrugged. "I can't afford to eat out all the time. Plus, I like it. I get into a rhythm in the kitchen, and it's pretty Zen. Relaxing even."

"I'm all for anything that puts a smile on your face. What are you going to make?"

"Would you like to walk down to the market and see what kind of fish have come in?"

"Oh man, that would be awesome." Ryan smiled, remembering trips to the fish market when he was a little boy, how he would stare wide-eyed at the live fish and crustaceans in their tanks. "I used to go there as a kid."

"Yeah? Did you pick out your own lobster and name him before your folks broke the news that he was going to be dinner?"

"Right, like we could afford lobster. Naw, we'd go get shrimp or crab for special occasions. But I liked to *watch* the lobster when I was a kid."

"Well, let's go relive some of your youth." Trey stretched and stood, and Ryan started hunting around for his clothes. It was very different from the last time he'd woken up at Trey's house—and not just because he wasn't hungover. He'd gotten comfortable with Trey's easygoing affection. What was it Trey had said? *"Leave each other better than we found each other."* Trey had already remodeled something in Ryan—made him more confident and assured. Would the newfound confidence linger when he returned to LA to find work? Maybe, maybe not. But he owed it to himself—and to Trey—to try to hold on to it.

"Should we take the dog?" he asked as he slipped his feet into his sandals.

"Nah. He had a long walk this morning. He needs his beauty sleep."

The walk to the fish market was only about a half mile along the beach, and Ryan filled it by describing his conversation with Ali that morning. "So she's coming here, and she's going to stay with me."

"I bet you're looking forward to having her here." Trey peered out at the ocean, a line forming between his brows.

"I'm looking forward to introducing you two. I think you'll like her."

The line disappeared from Trey's forehead, and he smiled. "I'm sure I will." He picked up Ryan's hand and gave it a squeeze, dropping it right away when Ryan glanced over his shoulder. "Sorry. I didn't think about your paparazzi situation."

Ryan shrugged. "I was at your house all afternoon. I was photographed half-naked on your front steps. I doubt a hand squeeze is much to make a fuss about."

"Does the press know you're gay?" Trey asked, almost too casually.

"Well, I'm not gay."

"Excuse me?" Trey stopped dead in his tracks. "Putting your dick in my ass a few hours ago seems pretty gay to me."

Ryan rolled his eyes and kept walking. Yeah, he'd had this conversation with every guy he'd ever dated. When Trey caught up, he said, "I'm bi, and I haven't had a long-term boyfriend or girlfriend since I've been living in LA, so it never seemed worth the trouble of coming out. I let people assume I'm straight, but I don't care if they know I like guys too. My publicist would care *how* they found out though. And it might affect the kind of jobs I could get."

"Huh. Bi. I never would have guessed."

"Really?"

"I haven't seen you look twice at a girl since I met you."

That made Ryan laugh as they approached the door to the fish market, which he held open for Trey. "Why would I look twice at anyone else when I'm with the hottest guy on Banker's Shoals?"

The expression on Trey's face as he stumbled through the door was absolutely priceless.

As they walked back to the house with a Styrofoam cooler full of fresh-caught grouper, Trey muddled over what Ryan had said. *The hottest guy on Banker's Shoals?* He peeked over at Ryan, who was *easily* the most beautiful person he'd ever met in his life, and something warm crashed around his insides like the waves on the shore.

"You think I'm hot?" he blurted.

Ryan smiled one of his gorgeous, charming grins. "Um, yeah? Have you seen yourself in the mirror?"

"Yeah, I have a broken nose, a lumpy ear, and red hair."

Biting his lip, Ryan reached over and flicked the lumpy ear. "Like I said, hot. Though I'd call you strawberry-blond more than a true redhead."

Just then, Ryan's phone buzzed, and he pulled it out of his pocket and grinned. "Hold on, it's Ali." His thumbs flew over the screen as he texted her back, their walk slowing to a crawl. Then he frowned at Trey.

"She's chartered a flight, but she's coming into the Outer Banks at lunchtime two weeks from Monday. And it's tech week."

"So?"

Ryan shoved his phone back in his pocket. "Her license is suspended. A couple months before she went into rehab, she got pulled over—high as a kite and driving *my* car—and she had coke in the glove box. Part of her plea deal was surrendering her driver's license for two years—not that that stopped her from driving." Ryan frowned. "She crashed West's car about six weeks later."

"I see."

"She's not a bad person—she just . . ." Ryan shrugged. "I can't make excuses for her. Hollywood was hard, and Ali doesn't know how to be hard back. And now I have to ask Mason if I can be late to rehearsal. During tech week."

Trey winced. That would literally be the worst thing Ryan could do. "Dude. You can't."

"I know. Especially now that Mason and I are finally getting along . . ." Ryan shrugged. "Maybe she can get a car service out to Banker's Shoals. I don't know."

"Why don't I pick her up for you?"

"You would do that?"

"Sure. I don't mind. And I get to talk her into spilling all your dirty secrets."

Ryan laughed. "She wouldn't dare—we pinky swore on that shit." Then his face grew serious. "Thank you so much, Trey. It means a lot to me that you would do that for me. And for her. She's a really special person."

What would it take to get Ryan's face to go soft like that when he mentioned Trey? "Anytime. Come on, let's go cook some fish."

Ryan, it turned out, knew next to nothing about cooking, but was an enthusiastic assistant. He heated and cleaned the grill to Trey's exacting specifications while Trey prepped the fish in a spicy citrus marinade. Together, they made a pico de gallo from the early tomatoes in Trey's garden and the mango going soft on his countertop.

"There should be a package of corn tortillas in the pantry, will you check?" Trey asked as he diced the onions for the pico.

"Found it." Ryan held them up.

"Great, wrap ten of them in two aluminum foil packets—we're going to heat them on the grill while the fish cooks. I'm afraid I don't have red cabbage, but there's some slaw mix in the vegetable drawer."

Ryan went digging and found the bag. "Got it."

"Is it any good?"

"How do you tell?"

"Are there brown spots on it? Liquid in the bag? Is it wilty and soft or crisp?"

"Crisp, no liquid, no brown spots."

That was a relief. "Awesome, put half of that in a bowl and stir in the marinade that I didn't put in with the fish."

"Yes, chef," Ryan teased.

"You got a Gordon Ramsay fetish I don't know about?" Trey shot back, grinning.

"Mmm, redheads."

Trey snapped a dishtowel at him, then looked around, taking stock of their feast. Pico de gallo and slaw for toppings. Corn tortillas and fresh grouper. Well, it would have to do. "I wish we had some avocado," he fretted.

"Too early in the season." Ryan made a face. "And there's nothing worse than bruised avocados shipped from god-only-knows-where. Trust me, I'm from California." His easygoing cackle filled Trey's kitchen and made Trey's heart twist and flop in his chest. He never could have imagined weeks ago that the laugh that had drawn his attention in Kim's bar would come to mean so much, or sound so good here in his home.

"Oh my god, you are such a dork," Trey teased, desperate to cover his sudden sentimentality with more laughter.

"Don't tell the tabloids," Ryan stage-whispered, then leaned in for a kiss, which Trey was all too happy to give him. Okay, so maybe he hadn't meant to shove Ryan up against the counter with such force they knocked the bowl of vegetable scraps for compost to the floor, and maybe he hadn't meant to carry Ryan back to the bedroom and blow him until he cried out Trey's name breathlessly and tugged his hair.

So what if the grouper marinated a little extra long while Ryan blew him right back, smiles in his eyes and the devil in his tongue?

By the time the fish went on the grill, they were both starving and sated, and they couldn't stop giggling at each other when their eyes met. Trey couldn't remember ever laughing like this with a lover before, and it felt so damned good it physically hurt.

"Oh my gaaah," Ryan sighed around the first bite of his taco. "Okay, dude, I lived in California for years and never had a fish taco that tasted like this. Did you put crack in it?"

"Nah. I put lu-uh-uuuhve in it." Trey waggled an eyebrow.

"That can't be it, I totally rinsed my mouth in between." Ryan smirked back, and they both started laughing again.

"You have the sense of humor of a twelve-year-old," Trey said when he could speak.

"You wouldn't have me any other way."

But that wasn't true—at this point, he'd take Ryan any which way he could get him—whether that meant laughing, silly, twelve-year-old-sense-of-humor Ryan, or the serious, careful Ryan who had driven him home from the bonfire and offered to get a cleaning service to purge his garage.

He was falling head over heels for both Ryans—and he only hoped he would be able to let them go at the end of the summer without a big empty Ryan-shaped hole taking over his heart.

Chapter Fifteen

The two weeks leading up to tech week passed in a blur of rehearsals, meals grabbed on the go, and late-night visits or calls to Trey. Mind-blowing sex followed by hours of talking about everything that mattered to them and some things that didn't. Trey told Ryan that his name was actually Patrick Donovan III, but that no one ever called him Patrick; Ryan confessed that having two names—a personal one and a professional one—sometimes made him feel like he lived two separate lives. When Ryan talked about growing up a willful only child, Trey described being the only boy in a family full of outspoken women—including his three sisters, one of whom had moved to Banker's Shoals while he was recovering from his injuries in the hospital. Ryan was used to creating small, intense, and transitory families on set and on stage. Something about his connection with Trey—though every bit as ephemeral—struck some deep place in his psyche he hadn't known was crying out to be loved. Trey seemed to hunger for a lightness that Ryan found easy to give—and Trey gave him back depths he didn't recognize in himself until Trey pointed them out.

Whenever he could, Ryan got up early to run—and "run into" Trey and Ferdinand on the beach. The weather was growing hotter and tourists were starting to pour into Banker's Shoals in a steady stream. Ryan was beginning to be recognized—and photographed—regularly, so his morning runs were often cut short to sign an autograph or pose for a selfie. He didn't *mind*—he loved the little bit of fan service he could give—but he was starting to crave alone time with Trey, and time was the one thing he was now running low on. With the sets mostly constructed and painted, Trey was rarely at the theater. On the bright side, Ryan's face—and other body parts—had remained absent from the pages of the *Herald*. Maybe his paparazzi stalker had given up.

On the Thursday before tech week, he texted Trey: *My last free weekend—wanna go somewhere?*

Trey's reply was a surprise. *Camping.*

Ryan had never dialed a phone so fast in his life.

"Yes, I said camping," Trey answered.

"You mean, like, tents and no showers and stinky buttholes, because that's not what I had in mind."

"Not exactly. Have you ever been camping before?"

"Once, with my Cub Scout troop when I was a kid. It was a memorable—if not pleasant—experience." Ryan shuddered. Ryan hadn't been scouting material; he'd been a little too afraid of the dark and a lot too mouthy to the authority figures.

"Can you give me access to West's backyard for a few hours tomorrow?"

"We're backyard camping? Like little kids?"

"Consider it glamping. Your girl Ali would approve."

Somehow, Ryan doubted that.

"Okay, show up before I leave for rehearsal tomorrow, and I'll give you the codes to the security system. I'm not sure about this glamping stuff, but it's our last weekend together; I'm going to trust you."

"All I've ever wanted," Trey teased. "Am I gonna see you tonight?"

Ryan sighed. "I wish. Rehearsal for *Much Ado* is probably going to run late. You know Zach Evers?"

"I tiled his kitchen backsplash."

"He's our Benedick understudy, and David got salmonella poisoning two nights ago, so they've got him down at OBH in Nags Head until he stops puking blood and the health department can pinpoint where he got it and notify the public."

"Poor David."

"Right? I've never seen a man's skin turn that shade of green. I thought he had appendicitis or kidney stones or something before he started butchin' it."

"Oh, gross. So, Zach is fumbling through a full rehearsal in role?"

"Well, he's doing all right if today was any indication. He's got excellent timing—but you know Mason."

"Yeah, I know Mason."

"So unless Dave miraculously recovers *and* makes the drive up highway twelve in record time, it's going to be a late night."

"How is Zach in the role?"

"Not as bad or as good as some of the other choices. I would play it differently, but that's the beauty of live theater. No two actors approach a role the same."

"You really don't mind not playing the lead?"

"Why would I mind? Don Pedro is an excellent role. So much meat to chew there. He's in the middle of all the matchmaking plots and schemes. Not to mention, he's the man everyone turns to for wisdom."

"I guess I don't understand how someone ambitious enough to move across the country to be a movie star is perfectly happy letting someone else lead the show."

Ryan smiled, even though Trey couldn't see it, because the common misunderstanding opened up an opportunity to geek out about his passion. "It's not a lack of ambition—it's . . . it's respect for the craft. Each role is important, or it wouldn't be there—I'm an actor, not an ego. I have as much respect for the role of Dogberry as I do for Don Pedro—more because Dogberry requires impeccable comic timing and a flair for slapstick, which is harder than it looks."

Trey's low laugh filled the line. "I get it. Picking an actor for a role is like picking a piece of wood for carpentry. Most of the world will never see the sides of the drawers, but it's worth picking the best piece you can so it will slide smoothly. Any art worth doing is worth doing beautifully."

Yeah. Trey *did* get him.

"That's a perfect analogy. Shit, as much as I'd love to talk your ear off about theater all day, I've got to get going. Mason wants me back at rehearsal at one. You're coming over in the morning?"

"Yes. Call me tonight, even if it's late. I sleep better after hearing your voice these days."

Ryan's heart fluttered in his chest. That was probably the nicest thing anyone had ever said to him.

"I will. Talk to you later."

"Later."

Ryan buzzed Trey through the gate just after six. Trey had been hoping to get to spend a little bit of time together, but Ryan was already on his way out to rehearsal. He stopped in the driveway for a long, leisurely kiss up against the side of Trey's pickup truck though, and Trey was all too happy to indulge him. Trey shoved a hand into Ryan's hair and pressed the length of their bodies together, rutting against him until they were both hard. He slid his other hand under Ryan's shirt, twisting and teasing at a nipple until Ryan let out a soft whimper of pleasure.

Cupping Ryan low, he whispered, "Too bad you have to go to rehearsal. Me, I got nothing but time. Maybe I'll set up our camping experience and then edge myself all day until you get home."

"You fucking bastard." Ryan groaned. "This is so unfair."

"Awww, but I'll be thinking of you. Thinking about the way you laugh, and those hot noises you make when you come. Mmm. And now I bet you'll be thinking about them all day too."

"I hate you." Ryan leaned forward and bit Trey's lower lip. "At least take a video for me if you do."

Trey laughed against Ryan's lips as they kissed again, then he let go of the fistful of hair he was still clutching. "Go on, get to rehearsal. Miss me."

"I fucking will." Ryan climbed back into the Volvo, extended his middle finger out the window, and started to drive away.

"I'll miss you too!" Trey called after him, grinning so hard he thought it would split his face. As soon as the gate closed behind Ryan, Trey let Ferdy out of the truck, grabbed his equipment, and got to work. Setting the campsite up by himself would take some time, and everything had to be perfect when Ryan got back at the end of the day. For the next six weeks, Ryan would be performing almost every night as well as every Sunday afternoon, so this really was their last free weekend together, and Trey wanted to make it memorable.

Ryan was on his way out of the theater when Annsley stopped him with a hand on his arm. He tried not to snap as he turned around—he *needed* to get to Trey, and rehearsal had run late.

"Hey, Ann, what's up?"

She didn't let go of his arm. "Are you coming to the party tonight?"

He groaned inwardly." Another one?"

"When did you get so antisocial?"

Gently moving her hand, he put on his most charming smile. "I'm not being antisocial. I've just got other plans. I've been seeing somebody, and this is our last chance to spend a weekend together before performances start."

Her eyes got wide. "Who? I thought you were dating Ali Parker."

"A townie. And no, Ali was my roommate in LA."

"A townie, huh? Someone from the play—someone on the crew? Oooh, is it Viki?"

"No, it's not Viki, and I'm not playing twenty questions. I'm going to go spend the weekend with my lover, and I'll see you Monday at tech."

"You're no fun!" she called after him.

"I am well aware!"

Though, he hoped Trey would disagree with her assessment. Because whatever Trey had planned for Ryan promised to be something he'd never forget, especially if that kiss in the driveway was any indication of what was in store for him.

Goddamn it, that had been hot. As he drove home, Ryan let himself remember Trey's fist clutching his hair as they'd kissed, the hard body pinning him against the side of the truck. Heat flashed through his body, and his dick stiffened in his jeans. Maybe it would be best if they could skip dinner and move straight to whatever glamping was.

The short drive across the island had never seemed to take so long before. And then once he arrived—had West's driveway gate always been this slow? It was taking forever to open. When it finally stopped, he pulled forward and up the drive. Trey's truck was still where he'd left it that morning, but Trey and Ferdy were nowhere to be seen. Damn.

Ryan parked next to the Ferrari, closed the garage door, and made his way inside. "Hello? Trey?"

No answer.

Dropping his keys in the bowl in the mudroom, he continued into the kitchen. No Trey. But a handwritten note, propped on a sweating bottle of prosecco, had his name in Trey's blocky script.

Ry,

I noticed you haven't been drinking lately. If you want to, bring this down to the backyard with you. If not, no worries. I have other refreshments waiting. Go take a shower and put on something comfortable.

Trey

Go take a shower. Well, all right, then.

Ryan bypassed the guest bathroom he usually used and made his way to West's gorgeous master bath. Slate tile and cedar paneling gave the room a rustic, masculine elegance he loved, and a giant copper bathtub was gathering patina in a corner. Ryan skipped the tub and headed straight for the glass-enclosed shower with its half-dozen sprayers and overhead rain spout. He massaged sandalwood soap into his tired muscles and let the hot water soothe him and loosen his limbs. He was still hard, but he tried to ignore that as much as possible, cleaning himself with the lightest touch. Since there was a good chance Trey would top the hell out of him tonight, he paid extra attention to his ass, enjoying the butterflies of anticipation that preparing himself for his lover stirred.

Oh god.

He dried himself with a decadently fluffy towel and considered the rest of Trey's note as he made his way back to the guest room. *"Put on something comfortable."* Pulling on a pair of briefs, he weighed his options. He could go out in his underwear, true. But the mosquitoes would probably have him covered in welts by the time he got down the steps to the backyard.

He ended up wearing a pair of flannel pajama pants that were so old they were worn soft and had fraying hems, and an equally ancient long-sleeved raglan.

When he reached the kitchen, he stared at the bottle of prosecco. He hadn't officially quit drinking or anything like that. But he hadn't had a drink in a few weeks, so maybe he should just skip the wine? But would that be making some kind of statement? He'd been the party guy for so long, he wasn't sure who he was without that identity. But if he quit drinking because he was scared of losing control, did that mean he was an alcoholic? Or just scared of being one? And did it matter if the end result was the same? He wasn't sure he even knew what drinking in moderation was anymore. Less than the guy next to you but more than the girl next to him didn't seem like the best metric, no matter how well it had worked in the past.

He left the bottle of prosecco on the counter, and stepped outside, into another world.

Trey had hung lanterns on the path leading down to the beach access, but before they got to the gate, there was a huge round tent and a portable fireplace off to one side. And . . . was that *music*? Trey was sitting on a lawn chair by the fire in red shorts and a plaid button-down, but he stood as Ryan approached.

"Hi."

"Hi. This is—this is gorgeous."

"Thank you. Wait until you see inside the yurt."

"Yurt?"

Trey gestured at the tent. "Yurt."

Cool. Ryan had never heard of a yurt before, but this thing was impressive. He followed as Trey pushed the mosquito netting away from the door and when he saw the inside, his jaw dropped. Holy shit there were hardwood floors and a bed—and the music he'd heard outside was playing through speakers hung on the rafters.

"This is— How did you do this in one day?"

Trey laughed. "It's totally portable. The bed is an air mattress on a platform. The floor rolls up. The speakers are a Bluetooth worksite system. I built it a few years ago—maybe I needed a blanket fort. Maybe I just needed something to do with my hands. It's special to me. And I wanted to share it with you."

Ryan turned around in a circle, taking in the beauty of Trey's craftsmanship. "It's amazing. Thank you for sharing it with me."

"Thank you for— Oh hell. I don't know. Everything?" Trey grabbed Ryan's hand and pulled him close. "What you did for me, with my garage—I can't even explain what it means to me. You blanket-forted me."

Ryan swallowed. There was a hard lump in his throat. "I was— You're welcome."

"Come here."

It wasn't as simple as an order given, an order followed. It wasn't complicated either. Trey called, and Ryan answered, with all the turmoil in his brain, the lust in his body, and the seemingly boundless affection Trey could pull from his heart.

Their lips met in the softest kiss they'd ever shared. Trey's fingertips skimmed Ryan's cheekbones, then down the sides of his face before one strong hand gripped his chin and tilted him *just so*.

Ryan's knees went weak, and he gripped Trey's shirt with both hands, needing to ground himself to this moment with this man. He groaned into Trey's mouth, fists opening and closing convulsively in Trey's shirt. "Need you."

"I'm here," Trey whispered.

"Need you to be rough and toppy and teasing like this morning." Ryan practically whined out the words, but when Trey smiled and bit behind his ear, he knew it was *on*.

"Take your clothes off and lie faceup on the bed."

Ryan shuddered and started tugging off his T-shirt.

"Slower."

Trey's voice hit him like a freight train, and he stood, heart pounding, in the middle of the yurt with his arms over his head, trapped in the shirt, blinded by it.

Then he felt Trey's hands on his chest.

At first the caresses were gentle, more of a languorous rub than anything else, but the pressure built and then fingers twisted his nipples, and his dick leaped in his pants.

"Fuck, Trey, *Fuck*."

Trey's hands disappeared from his chest, pulled the shirt back over Ryan's face, exposing him, but he didn't care. He liked how Trey saw him. Instead of stripping the shirt from Ryan's arms, Trey tugged and wrapped and twisted it until Ryan's hands were held together.

Holy shit.

Ryan had had plenty of nonmainstream sex—okay, so he'd had some threesomes-*ish* with Ali and West—but he didn't consider himself a bondage kind of guy. And yet, with Trey pinning his arms, his cock was as hard as it had ever been.

"Get on the bed," Trey growled.

Ryan got.

He stretched out on his back, leaving his arms above his head and grasping the headboard for dear life. Trey grabbed his pants and pulled them down his legs, briefs too. Tossing them aside, he abruptly spread Ryan's legs, putting his cock, balls, and ass on display.

Ryan groaned. He'd started to love topping Trey, but this . . . God, he craved this. Being manhandled, pushed around, teased, and tormented.

"I'm going to give you two choices."

Oh shit.

"I can blindfold you, and you'll never know what's going to happen next. Or I can show you everything I'm going to do to you before I do it."

Both ideas were hot. But . . ."Do I need a safeword?"

Trey stretched out on the bed next to him and ran a comforting hand along his chest. "'No' and 'stop' work for me. How about you?"

Relieved, Ryan nodded. "They work for me too. Only, I didn't know if we were getting into some kinky shit . . ."

A low laugh rumbled from Trey's chest, and he tugged one of Ryan's nipples. "More just bedroom games. I'm not about to break out the whips and chains on you."

"You have whips and chains?" Ryan's eyes widened.

"No. I don't. I have you in my bed, and I want to drive you crazy. So. What will it be? Blindfold? Or full knowledge?"

Jesus, that was a hard decision. On the one hand, if he was blindfolded, it would be easier to sink into sensation. But on the other? He could always fucking close his eyes.

"I want to know."

Trey's evilest laugh filled the tent, and Ryan wondered what he'd just signed himself up for.

"Leave your hands above your head. You can keep holding the headboard if you want."

Trey sat up on the bed, reached under it, and produced a big—really fucking big, damn, how much were they going to use tonight?—bottle of lube.

Ryan closed his eyes.

"Look at me." Trey's voice called him back, and of course his traitorous fucking eyes did as they were told. He watched, mesmerized, as Trey dumped some of the lube on his fingers, rolled it around, and pulled it apart in long, slick strings. It was weird, and a little gross, and devastatingly sexy all at once because he knew where that was going and . . . *damn*.

"Lift your legs."

This part was harder. Ryan lifted his knees to his chest. One of Trey's fingertips dipped at his hole, probing the outside. Ryan let out a shaky breath as two fingers slid inside him.

"Oh *god*."

Trey took his time, gently teasing and massaging while Ryan's cock grew impossibly harder. He rode Trey's fingers, loving the stretch and the pressure. When Trey brought his other hand up to tease Ryan's nipples, Ryan groaned and let his eyes slip closed again.

Trey's hands disappeared, and Ryan let out another low groan. But then Trey's mouth was on him, and his shoulders arched off the bed. Trey bit one side of Ryan's chest, then the other, then he moved down his body to mouth his cock, teasing with his lips first, then giving him a long, slow lick.

"I brought toys," Trey said, matter-of-factly, as if he were discussing a book he'd like Ryan to read.

"Oh?"

"Mmm. You said you love ass play, I figured why not?" A finger rubbed along Ryan's rim as Trey began to suck the tip of his cock.

Ryan's hips wouldn't lie still, instead pulsing up in short motions. Trey let go of Ryan's cock with a *pop*.

"What I'm wondering is, should I grab a big dildo and stretch you out? Or maybe a little glass number with a curve for teasing your prostate? So many possibilities for both."

Surely he didn't expect Ryan to choose? "Whatever . . . whatever you like."

Trey's grin was positively wicked. "Don't go anywhere."

Ryan lay back, his chest heaving, listening to Trey move about the yurt. He couldn't identify half the sounds, and he didn't care. Trey had promised to show him whatever he had in store.

When Trey came back, he kept his promise, holding up a slim, curved glass dildo.

"Frosted glass, nice," Ryan managed.

Trey smiled. "It's not frosted. It's been in the cooler."

Oh shit. That was all the warning Ryan got before Trey circled one nipple with icy-cold glass. His back arched, his skin seemed to tighten, and he shuddered all over. Was this pain? Pleasure? His dick throbbed, and his mouth dropped open on a wordless shout.

"Interesting," Trey murmured, then he did the same to the other nipple. This time, Ryan was somewhat prepared, and he managed to refrain from jumping out of bed, though he shivered at the cold touch.

But when Trey told him to lift his hips and slid a pillow under them, reality came crashing in. Ryan shook his head. "Not cold. I can't, sorry."

"Okay." Trey leaned over him and kissed him, long and slow, and he set the dildo aside. "Just kiss me awhile."

And, oh yeah, that was good. Trey's hands—still a little cold, but not icy like the dildo—sliding over his body, tugging his hair, they brought him back to that lush, wanton headspace where he was full of desire, sensation, and need. When Ryan's hips started rocking, Trey groaned and pulled out of the kiss. He picked up the dildo, tested it against his hand.

"It's not as cold now." He touched it to the side of Ryan's face. "Okay?"

Ryan nodded and closed his eyes. He felt Trey's light tap around his hole, and he dropped his legs wide. Trey teased him with his fingers, then the cold caress of glass pressed against him—and he pressed back. The hard, unyielding glass slid easily into his body, then Trey turned it, so the curve brought the tip right against his gland, and Ryan's whole world narrowed down to that gentle pressure. His head hit the pillow, his lips fell open, and hips rolled and thrust with

Trey's movements as he twisted and teased the glass in and out of Ryan's body.

On one particularly decadent grind against his gland, Ryan let out a low shout, and then, "Please. God, Trey, fuck me. I want you."

The glass dildo disappeared with a rough tug, and then Trey was over him, sliding inside, lips and hands everywhere.

"God, you're so beautiful, so good, Ryan. That was so hot."

"I'm not gonna last," Ryan groaned, shoving himself down on Trey's cock. "Jerk me, please."

Trey spit on his hand, wrapped it around Ryan's cock, and started jerking him, rough and fast, and Ryan couldn't take it anymore. After the whole day of anticipation, after Trey's power games and teasing, his body had reached the limit of how much pleasure it could endure.

The orgasm seemed to eclipse his entire body, starting in his groin and washing outward in hot bursts as he spurted everywhere. He managed to yank his eyes open to see Trey come, his lip between his teeth and his eyes scrunched shut as if he couldn't bear to feel *that good*.

For a long moment, Trey braced himself on shaking arms, breathing heavily until Ryan reached his still T-shirt-bound hands up, bending his elbows so he could put them around Trey's head and pull him down for a long, lush kiss.

"That was amazing. You're amazing," Ryan mumbled.

"Think you'll remember that?" Trey joked, nipping at his ear.

"Always."

Afterward, they roasted hot dogs and marshmallows over the fire—nothing fancy, but it provided plenty of opportunity for sausage jokes. They had the whole weekend together for fancy food—this night was perfect just as it was.

Chapter Sixteen

Trey knew what Ali Parker looked like—anyone who had walked through a grocery store line with a tabloid display had seen more of her than she probably intended. Despite Ryan's descriptions of her as sweet and kindhearted, Trey was still nervous when he got out of his truck at the airport, and he couldn't put his finger on why. At least, not until he realized that he wanted to make a good first impression on the one person Ryan loved most in all the world. But how did one make a good first impression on a movie star?

Inside the small FBO building, he gave the airport employee the tail number for Ali's plane and explained he was there to pick up a passenger. He'd never picked someone up at the tiny local airport before, more often driving all the way to Norfolk. He didn't know many people who could afford to charter a plane.

The man entered something into his computer and then nodded. "Drive to the gate, I'll open it for you. Once inside, follow the directions of the operator on the field."

He watched from inside his truck as the small charter plane landed on the runway, and the statuesque brunette descended the stairs. Something about how she moved was familiar—the stiff awkwardness to her gait. It wasn't until she reached the ground, wheeling her suitcase behind her, that he made the connection—she moved like Kim, well into her second trimester of pregnancy.

Holy shit.

He jumped out of the truck and headed toward her. When he got close enough, he extended a hand. "Ali? I'm Trey."

She smiled widely, pulling off her sunglasses and letting the full wattage of her stunning beauty hit him, then she bypassed his waiting hand to give him a hug. "Hi, Trey. It's so nice to meet you."

"It's nice to meet you too." He disentangled from her, trying to avoid looking at the now-obvious baby bump. Not that she was making any attempt to hide it. "Here, let me take your suitcase."

"Thanks." She handed over the wheeling suitcase. "Ryan said it's about an hour to the island. I can't tell you how much I appreciate your coming to meet me here."

"I'd do just about anything for Ryan," he confessed, then gestured toward his truck. "You're probably used to more glamorous transportation, but I did take a lint roller to the seats to get the dog hair out."

She laughed, a throaty chuckle that reminded him of Ryan. "I'm sure it's fine. Ryan texted me a photo of that beast you call a dog. I can't wait to meet him. I love animals."

Trey opened the door for her and offered a hand to help her climb in. When she was safely settled, he closed the door, then hoisted her suitcase into the bed of the truck and secured it with a strap.

The first twenty minutes of the drive, she was occupied with her phone—which seemed to ding constantly with incoming texts—checking voice mail, and he guessed, social media too. Weren't all the famous people on Instagram these days?

He took the opportunity of her distraction to study her in sideways glances. She was radiantly pretty, with huge brown eyes and skin glowing warm and tan. Even though he wasn't attracted to women, her beauty was captivating. As she swiped at her phone with one manicured thumb, she twisted a strand of hair around her finger and nibbled at the end. The effect was girlish and vulnerable, and Trey understood immediately what Ryan had meant when he said Ali didn't know how to be hard.

When she finally tucked her phone back into her purse, she flashed him a slightly-embarrassed smile. "Sorry. I didn't have free use of my phone for six weeks. It feels like the ultimate luxury now."

"How far along are you?" he asked.

"Didn't your mama ever teach you not to ask a lady that unless she tells you she's pregnant?"

He rolled his eyes. "Yeah, my mama did. But my sister is twenty-two weeks along, and you look pretty much the same."

"I'm only eighteen weeks." She turned her gaze to the ocean speeding past the window. "And if you do the math, you'll discover I was pregnant when I went to rehab. I didn't find out until I was nine weeks along, so I wasn't intentionally doing drugs while I was pregnant. That's *why* I went to rehab."

"I'm not judging you."

"Well, then you'll be the first and probably the last." She dropped her hand to her stomach and rubbed it absently. "I felt her move the other day. It felt like—like the weirdest gas. Isn't that funny?"

"My sister says the same thing." He smiled. "I'll introduce her to you, if you like. She's a little spitfire who owns a pub on the beach. That's where I met Ryan."

Her eyes widened. "I'd like that. I'm not ready to tell any of my friends back in California that I'm pregnant. That's part of why I'm here, to hide out with Ryan until I *am* ready. But it's been lonely going through all these milestones by myself."

"Does Ryan know? He didn't say anything to me."

She shook her head. "I haven't told him yet. He'll be fine with it though, don't you think?"

That depends on whether or not it's his.

The thought came to Trey out of nowhere, and he flushed red. He wasn't about to interrogate her, so he just nodded. "Yeah, I guess so? I mean, he's Ryan. I think he'll take anything in stride."

"He does. A lot of people don't take him seriously, but he's got really super amazing problem-solving skills. If he weren't an actor—and if he'd paid more attention in high school science classes—he could totally be a doctor."

Seeing how Ali clearly adored her best friend made Trey unexpectedly happy. The Ryan he'd met was full of life and laughter, but socially driftless without Trey or his friends in the theater. He could see already how Ryan and Ali had buffered the world for each other.

Ice broken, they talked about Ryan, the two plays, and of course Ferdinand, all along Highway 12 to Banker's Shoals. Ali lit up with laughter as Trey told her the story of Ryan's first morning at his house, Ferdy's underwear theft and all.

"Oh my god, poor Ryan!" Then she laughed so hard she snorted and started fanning herself with both hands. "Okay, no more funny stories, or I'm gonna wet myself."

"Don't worry, we're pulling into Banker's Shoals in about ten minutes." He pointed at the shoreline widening out in front of them. "Welcome to our little island."

Since he didn't have an access card to Ryan's gate, and Ryan was at rehearsal, Trey took Ali to his own home. She fawned over Ferdy, scratching his belly and cooing at him.

"I have to get to work, and Ryan's at tech rehearsal—it's going to be a long one. I'll probably be back here before him, but if you need anything, text me. Ryan gave you my number right?"

"All I need is about a gallon of water and a long nap." She laughed. "But I will definitely text you or Ryan if I need anything else."

"There's a Brita pitcher in the fridge, guest room is the first door on the left. Restroom is the next door down. If the dog scratches at the back door, or if he starts acting obnoxious, you can let him out back. Help yourself to whatever you want from the fridge."

She stood up and hugged him again. "Thank you, Trey. I appreciate you."

"Um, you're welcome."

Ryan was watching Annsley and a still-vaguely-green David verbally spar on stage as Beatrice and Benedick when his phone buzzed in his pocket. Trey.

We need to talk. Urgent. About Ali.

His heart sped up. What could possibly have happened? His brain started racing through various scenarios, each worse than the last.

He caught Mason's eye and gestured that he was going outside. Mason nodded, and he hurried out to the parking lot and called Trey.

As soon as Trey picked up, words started pouring out of Ryan. "What happened? Is she okay? Did something happen with the plane?"

"She's fine. I'm sorry. I didn't mean to scare you. It's not that kind of urgent."

"Not that kind of—" Ryan blew out a frustrated breath. "How many kinds of urgent are there? What happened?"

"This is really super not my place, as she would say, to mention."

"Okay. But you're going to anyway?"

"She's pregnant. Eighteen weeks."

Ryan sat down hard on the front steps of the theater. "Holy shit."

"I don't mean to pry, and this doesn't change anything between us, but is there any chance you're the father?"

That made Ryan laugh out loud. "No. Absolutely zero. I used to let her boyfriend fuck me while she watched, but that's as intimate as she and I have ever been."

"Okay, I believe you."

"You *believe* me? What's that supposed to mean? That because I'm bi, I'm some slut who can't keep it in my pants? She's a beautiful woman who I care about deeply, but you *believe* me when I said I didn't fuck her—how magnanimous of you."

"Oh for fuck's sake, I should *not* have told you."

"No, you shouldn't have, but you did, so now you and I need to have the conversation we're having. You get pretty fucking judgmental sometimes, and I don't need that kind of negativity from someone I'm seeing."

"You're right. I'm sorry. I don't always . . . I have a hard time believing someone like you would want to be with someone like me. And I get shitty when I feel bad. You don't deserve that. I'm truly sorry."

"I believe you."

Trey's soft laughter told Ryan he understood. "So, if you're not the father?"

Ryan scrubbed a hand over his face. "West Brady."

"Oh."

"Yeah. So, this will be fun."

The door to the theater opened, and David popped his head out. "Hey, man, better get in here before Mason loses his shit."

"Trey, I gotta go. Listen, if you get back to your house before I do—tell Ali you told me. I don't want her to be blindsided."

"I guess I deserve that."

"Yeah, you do. But Trey? I am actually glad you told me, even though it was really super not your place. Gotta go. See you tonight."

He hung up and returned to the stage just in time to hear his cue.

Hours later, he rang the doorbell at Trey's house, and Ferdinand barked and ran to the door. He braced himself when Trey opened the door and the dog came barreling through. Ferdy gave him a quick sniff all over, and then went running toward the kitchen.

Trey shrugged. "He likes Ali. A lot."

Ryan shut the door behind himself and gave Trey a quick kiss. "Thanks for everything today. She's in the kitchen?"

"Yeah. I'll take Ferdy for a walk so you two can have your reunion in private. Here, Peanut!"

Ali was standing up when Ryan came into the kitchen, and she threw her arms open wide for a hug. Ryan felt a lump rise in his throat at the sight of her, and he ran over and hugged her as hard as he could.

"Oh, Al." He stepped back and looked at her belly. "When are you gonna tell him?"

She laughed and hugged him again. "Hello to you too. God, I missed you."

"You dodged my question."

"I need to go in for an anatomy scan sometime in the next four weeks. Once I'm sure everything is okay with the baby, then I'll tell him—I know it's not ideal, but neither is finding out you're pregnant when you're an addict. I just want to know what, if anything, I'm facing before I ask him to face it with me."

"I can understand that—have the doctors said there's any reason to worry?"

She shook her head and folded her hands protectively over her belly. "They haven't—but I'm still scared. It's not just about me anymore."

"Wow, baby. You're totally somebody's mom."

Her eyes went wide and her smile soft, and she tucked a long brown curl behind her ear with one hand and rubbed her belly with the other. "Yeah."

"Are you ready to go to West's house?"

She nodded. "Yes. Can we make milkshakes and cuddle and watch old movies?"

"Definitely."

"Is your boyfriend going to come with us? I like him."

"No, but maybe he'll come over tomorrow. I'm glad you approve."

As they drove to West's house, Ali was uncharacteristically quiet, until she put a hand on Ryan's arm and asked, "Are you and Trey in love?"

"How do you know if you're in love with someone? I like him a lot, like he's a really great person, and I think he's incredibly sexy. And he makes me laugh—like the way you make me laugh. I just . . . what's *not* to love?"

"He said you were mad at him. That he fucked it up with you big time by telling my secret. Don't be mad at him for that, okay?"

"I'm not mad about that. I'm not even mad anymore at all. But I was mad because he sometimes says things that are hurtful—and he means to direct them at himself but they come back at me. When I told him you and I have never had sex, he was all 'I *believe* you.'"

Ali laughed. "Well, goober, you do call me baby and say you love me all the time. You can't expect everyone to understand."

"But if he trusts me—if he loves me—shouldn't he understand me?"

"I don't know the answer to that. West and I love each other like crazy, but sometimes he'll say something that makes me wonder how we grew up on the same planet. Then maybe I wonder if there's one world that's movies and plays—" she nudged his arm "—a world where everyone understands their part. And then there's another world where it's all chaos and no one was given a script, and that's where we live. Some of us are lucky enough to get to visit the one that makes sense."

Ryan pulled up to the gate and waved his card at the sensor until it started to slide open.

"I said almost that exact same thing to West at the beginning of the summer. Not as eloquently as you, but I'm not some fancy-pants screenwriter."

"West has only ever lived in the world that makes sense. Except maybe the night that Jason died. That was the first time his life didn't make sense. He was in love with Jason, you know."

"I didn't know."

"That's why I'm not quite ready to face him. I very nearly put him through that again."

And Ryan had nothing to say to that. Because he was still pissed at her for putting her life in danger too. Maybe someday he could be that bigger person who was grateful for the accident if it ended up being what got her sober. But he wasn't there yet, and his anger wouldn't help her.

Inside the house, he showed Ali to the master bedroom, then went to his own room, changed into his pajamas, and met her back in the living room.

"I'll go make milkshakes—you pick out a movie."

She nodded and grabbed the remote as he started toward the kitchen.

"Hey, Ryan?"

"Yeah?"

"I think it's okay if you and Trey don't always understand each other. There is no script. You don't get to rehearse being in love."

Chapter Seventeen

Having Ali in town, sober and silly and enchanting, felt to Ryan as if he had found something he'd forgotten he was looking for. He had no rehearsals scheduled for Wednesday—dress rehearsals would run Thursday and Friday—so they took the Ferrari and went shopping in Nags Head.

Ali, when shopping, was the most *Ali*.

She flirted shamelessly, tried on mountains of clothing, and cracked jokes about everything from the season's colors to whether her bump or her butt was growing faster. Three times, they were recognized and ended up signing autographs and posing for selfies with delighted sales assistants. When they arrived back at West's house for dinner, they were both happily exhausted. Ryan parked the car and started into the house ahead of Ali.

"How about when you asked that shoe guy if you could still safely wear stilettos in the third trimester—I thought he was going to have a panic attack!"

"Oh shit, Ryan. Shit. Shit. Shit. We are so goddamn stupid."

"What?" He turned around. Ali's eyes were wide, staring at her phone.

"Fuck, fucking shit, goddamn *Gossip Miner*!" she shouted, then burst into tears and pushed past him into the house. She walked straight to the freezer, grabbed the half gallon of ice cream, and tossed her phone on the counter with a force that made Ryan wince.

"Spoons are next to the sink." He pointed at a drawer, and she opened it hard enough to rattle the silverware inside. Then he picked up her phone and read the headline out loud.

"Bryan Hart Bisexual Baby Scandal."

Ali handed him a spoon.

"I think it's a little too early to tell if the baby is bisexual," he joked, mostly to hide his panic at being outed by *Gossip Miner* of all places.

Then he scrolled down.

In addition to Instagram photos of him and Ali in a maternity store with him resting what appeared to be a proprietary hand on her belly, there was a photo of Trey kissing the shit out of him out in the driveway. *Oops.*

"Baby, you're *out* now."

His stomach lurched. "Maybe we should call our boyfriends," he whispered.

"Who do you think sent me the link?"

He closed his eyes. There was no way Trey would have sent it to Ali and not him. Which meant—

"I'm sorry." He reached for the ice cream and took a bite.

"I can't believe we didn't ask people not to post the photos on social media."

"Who'd have thought we would do something even dumber sober than we did when we were getting fucked up all the time?"

"I should call him, I guess. This is *so* not how I wanted him to find out."

"Call him. I'll make milkshakes."

When she disappeared upstairs, Ryan texted Trey. *Are you out? I mean, like, out to the world out?*

I was Vermont-married to another man for several years. I'm out. Why?

Ryan took a deep breath and forced himself not to cringe as he sent the link to the *Gossip Miner* article.

Trey's reply was nearly instantaneous.

How can an unborn baby be bisexual?

Then a moment later: *Are you okay? I'm here for whatever you need.*

I'll be fine. I just—damn dude. I'm so glad I didn't out you.

Ali came downstairs ten minutes later, puffy-eyed and sniffling. "He's going to charter a plane. He'll be here tomorrow."

"You don't seem happy about that." Ryan handed her the milkshake he'd made for her.

"Yeah, well. How the fuck was I supposed to know he had a Google alert on my name monitored by some assistant? I didn't want him to find out until I knew everything was okay."

"Okay, I get that. But, baby, it's his kid too. If everything's not okay, don't you think he deserves to know that?"

"Of course he does. But I thought maybe— I don't know what I thought. It all made sense before and now nothing does."

"Come here." He wrapped his arms around her. "You're gonna be okay. West is fine. You'll find out together whether everything is okay with the baby, and that's how it should be. I love you."

"I love you too."

"Will you be all right if I go call Trey?"

She nodded. "Then can we do collagen masks and pedicures in front of *Breakfast at Tiffany's*?"

"Abso-fucking-lutely."

When Trey and Ryan entered the theater Thursday afternoon— an hour early, so Ryan could confess his sins to Mason—the sound of a loud argument carried down the hallway from the office. They glanced at each other, then at the office door.

"Should we?" Ryan asked.

Trey didn't like the idea of interrupting Caro and Mason in the middle of an argument—especially if it was another argument about Ryan—but if Ryan didn't tell Mason about the *Gossip Miner* article before rehearsal, there would be hell to pay.

"I've got your back. Lead on."

I'm sending him into the lion's den.

Ryan knocked on the door and then pushed it open without waiting for a response. Trey followed him into the room.

"Hey, guys, what's up?" Ryan asked.

Caro wiped at her eyes, and Mason glared. "Do you want to tell them?"

"Our advance ticket sales for the season are way down. From the looks of things, this is going to be the last season of Shakespeare by the Sea. Mason and I are trying to figure out what to do next.

Dissolving the company, etc. I think we should wait until after the season to make any permanent decisions. He disagrees."

Trey remembered the other argument he'd interrupted, the one Caro had won. Mason had been resentful—and not altogether sold on her reasoning. Why hadn't they capitalized on Ryan's presence if it had gotten this bad?

Ryan sat down, eyes wide with shock. "Wow. What are you going to do? You can't just—you can't just close the theater."

"Honey, I know you love this place as much as we do. But we can't stay open at an operating loss." Caro took his hand. "I'm sorry. I know this is a shock."

"Are you sure there's nothing else you can do? Can I, I don't know, buy in financially? Be a silent partner somehow?"

"It's too late for that." Mason glanced over at Caro. "Anyway, why are you here so early? Call isn't for another hour."

"Wait, hold on—what do you mean by too late? The season hasn't even started. Maybe if we, I don't know, put posters up? Or took out a radio ad?"

"Ryan," Trey put a hand on his shoulder, "let the grown-ups sort this."

He regretted the words instantly. Ryan's face went blotchy and red, and his hands tightened into fists.

"Ry—"

"Excuse me," Ryan cut Trey off and stood slowly, smoothly, the only sign of his distress the tension in his jaw and the color on his face. "Mason, I'll see you in an hour."

He left the room with his chin held high, and Trey stood frozen, helpless. What had he just done?

As soon as the door shut behind Ryan, Mason turned on Trey. "What the fuck is wrong with you?"

"You so blew it." Caro shook her head.

"I didn't mean— I was just joking. Shit."

"That young man has grown up more in the last eight weeks than he had in the eight years before that," Mason seethed. "And now that you've pissed him off, he'll run out and do something stupid."

Unfair. But Trey could hardly call Mason out for being unfair to Ryan after what *he'd* just said.

"He won't do anything stupid. I keep fucking up the things that should be dead simple. I'll apologize to him. I'll make it right, I promise."

"See that you do."

Trey turned to Caro. "You know, you could probably still turn this around if you used his name in the advertising."

"No." Caro shook her head. "Absolutely not."

"Why the fuck not? He is *so* willing to help you."

"Because I'm not taking away his last shot!" Caro exploded. "Even guys like my cousin—talented, good-looking guys—they only get one shot at Hollywood. *If* he's lucky enough to get a second chance when he goes back to LA, that is *it* for him. If word gets around that he's slumming it here in North Carolina . . ."

"He is *not* slumming it," Trey said.

"Thank you," Mason muttered.

"No. We aren't exploiting him." Caro stood up and left the office. The door was on a hydraulic hinge so it couldn't slam, but the soft *whoosh* as it closed behind her was every bit as final.

Ryan left the theater in a daze of pain and petulance. Was that really what Trey thought of him? That he couldn't handle business conversations? That he was a child? He had thought Trey, of all people, was different from the people who wrote him off as shallow.

He made it down to the beach and out onto the pier before he reached for his phone and called the only person he could think of.

"Hiya, Rya."

"Hey, Al. How are you?"

"I'm freaking out. How did things go at the theater?"

"Freaking out—why?"

"I haven't seen West in over two months and I'm scared and what if it's really over? What if he doesn't want me back—if he doesn't love me anymore? What if I'm a terrible mother?"

"You're going to be a great mother. West loves you. Whether or not you guys get back together, he loves you."

"Ugh, why is my life such a soap opera?"

"I'm not answering that question." Ryan chuckled. Even freaking out, Ali could make him feel better.

"You didn't answer my other one either. About the theater."

"I didn't get a chance to tell them. I'm probably the least of their worries, anyway. They're having financial problems."

"Oh, Ryan. I'm sorry sweetie."

"Yeah. It sucks." Desperate to change the subject, he asked, "What time is West coming into town?"

"His plane lands at nine tonight. He's trying to arrange a car service, but a lot of them don't run that late or are already booked. I guess the busy season has started."

"I'll be in rehearsal until at least eight thirty. No way I can get to the mainland in time." He frowned. "Please tell me you aren't thinking of driving out there to pick him up."

Silence hung over the line. Finally, Ali cleared her throat. "I'm going to pretend you didn't say that."

Ryan winced. He'd just done the same thing to Ali that Trey had done to him. "I'm sorry. I'm in a pissy mood. I have dress rehearsal in an hour for *Julius Caesar*. Text me if you can't work something out—if all else fails, he can stay in a hotel on the mainland and I can go get him tomorrow morning."

"Break a leg at dress. Don't worry about West. He's a big boy and can find his own transportation to the island. Love you."

She hung up.

Ryan's hand balled into a useless fist at his side. A seagull landed nearby and pecked at a splotch of peeling paint.

"I'm so tired of being useless," Ryan said softly, his voice swallowed up by the waves.

The seagull cocked its head, pecked at the dock again, and then flew away.

"Yeah, fuck you too."

He shoved his phone in his pocket, ignoring the vibration of a text notification. There was literally nobody in the world he wanted to talk to at the moment. A new low for the party guy.

Ryan was irritable all through dress, but thankfully he could play Antony in his sleep—and throw all his futile rage into Antony's impassioned speeches rather than at his castmates. Mason tried to pull him aside during the intermission break, but blanched when Ryan glowered at him.

By the time they rehearsed the curtain call, his mood had gone from furious to sullen and withdrawn. The rest of the cast was hugging and clapping while he stood, arms folded over his chest, and waited to be dismissed.

Mason came onto the round stage and raised both hands to get their attention. "Thank you, everyone, for your time tonight. I'll see you tomorrow night for dress for *Much Ado*, 6 p.m. Ryan, I need to speak with you before you go."

A bitter growl ripped from Ryan's throat as he pushed past Mason and stomped to the office. He couldn't take one of Mason's bullshit for-his-own-good sermons right now. Mason followed him and closed the door gently.

"I saw the *Gossip Miner* headline. Are you okay?"

"Wait, what?" Ryan whirled around and stared at Mason. He'd expected a lecture at the least, a dressing down at the most, not . . . concern? "Who are you and what have you done with my friend?"

"You've been outed—publicly, in the media—in a flagrant disregard for your choice or your privacy. Then you came to my office and were blindsided by the news of the theater closing, and your boyfriend insulted you in front of your family." Mason made a small, helpless gesture with his hands. "I'm worried about you."

"It's not like I was going to be able to hide that I like men forever. As for the rest of it . . ." Ryan's shoulders slumped as the bitterness that had kept him on edge all evening rushed out of him. "Are you okay?"

Mason nodded, glancing around the room. "We were hoping that selling my house would reduce my debt enough that I could get another business loan to cover the rest of the operating costs. But I can't make it happen in time."

Ryan wrapped a brotherly arm around Mason's shoulders without even thinking about it. He was a tactile person, used to touching and holding the people he cared about—but Mason was *not* a hugger.

Mason stiffened a moment, and then let himself be held. "I'm going to fucking miss the hell out of this place."

"I'm so sorry, man."

"Me too." Mason flinched in his arms, as if admitting that was a weakness. "But at least you got to be here for the final season. You played Antony in your very first role here, and you'll be the very last Antony to take this stage—that's poetic, right?"

A lump rose in Ryan's throat, and he tried to force it away. "I can't imagine Banker's Shoals without the playhouse. It's like Banker's Shoals without you or Caro."

"Caro and I aren't going anywhere. You'll always have family on Banker's Shoals."

And despite the anger and bitterness that had been twisting him up inside all afternoon, something else washed over Ryan: gratitude and love all wrapped up together. He wasn't sure how, but he wanted to give that feeling back to Mason and Caro. He shuddered and clung closer to Mason, who hugged him back like a brother—with comfort and solidarity.

Maybe the theater situation was hopeless—but what if it wasn't? Didn't he owe it to Mason and Caro to help them the way they helped him, if he could? If they wouldn't readily accept financial help—maybe there was another way.

Ryan left the theater that night resolved not to give up on Shakespeare by the Sea—not yet, and not until he had exhausted every possibility.

Chapter Eighteen

Trey slammed the door of his truck as he climbed into the cab. Seriously, *fuck* Doc Wharton.

He wanted to punch a wall—to take out this blistering rage on something that wouldn't break under his fury. Instead, he rested his forehead on the steering wheel, took a series of deep breaths, and let out a low growl of frustration.

He hadn't left the therapist's office angry in months. He didn't feel like a million bucks after most sessions, but this anger and shame was so much more potent than the usual emotional and physical depletion he carried home with him from therapy.

The last thing she said to him before he'd left rang in his ears. *"I know you're angry, and I think you should ask yourself why."*

Goddamn doublespeaking. She *knew* why he was angry.

His phone buzzed in his pocket. He dug it out—maybe it was Ryan. But no. *Kim.*

How was therapy? xo

He glared at the wall of the building, then let out a sigh and texted back. *Sucked. Bad session.*

The phone started ringing within seconds. Damn it. "What do you want?"

"Come over and tell your favorite sister all about it. I'm a bartender; there's nothing I haven't heard before."

"It's Thursday night—you guys get so busy on Thursdays."

"Yup. And your barstool is empty right now, but I don't anticipate it staying that way for long."

"I'm okay."

"I'll believe it when I see it. Come on, don't make your pregnant sister beg. You haven't come by in weeks. I miss you."

And that, of course, was Kim playing dirty. He *had* been occupied with Ryan, and he'd been neglecting his family, and Kim knew he knew it.

"Fine. I'll be there in a few."

"I love you."

"Yeah, yeah. Love you too."

Ten minutes later, Trey walked through the door of the bar—which was already packed with tourists—and straight to the barstool he had been sitting on the night he met Ryan. The one next to the beer taps, where he could chat with, yeah, his favorite sister, while she worked.

"Well, hi there, stranger." She grinned at him and tapped him a glass of beer. "What brings you here tonight?"

"Nosy, no good, meddling sister."

"She sounds awful." Kim wrinkled her nose.

"She's all right," he drawled, trying to hold back his own grin. The anger left over from his therapy appointment was already slipping away, leaving him tired and drawn thin. "Pushy, though."

"So what happened?" Kim folded her arms over her chest.

"I was a dick to my boyfriend."

Admitting it like that was a weight off his shoulders, but one look at Kim's scowl had him hanging his head.

"Why? I thought he was pretty awesome?"

"He is. And I texted him an apology right away. He's in rehearsal now, or I'd be groveling in person, if he let me."

"So, you were a dick to him because . . .?"

He sighed. "According to Doc Wharton, I don't think I deserve to be happy so I'm sabotaging my own relationship rather than dealing with my secret feelings of shame. Or something."

"Uh-huh." Kim nodded. "Sounds about right to me."

Trey recoiled. "What the fuck? I thought you were on my side?"

"Of course I am. Are *you* on your side?"

What kind of question was that? "Who else's side would I be on?"

Kim hung her bar towel over a hook behind the bar and came around the side. Hoisting herself onto the barstool next to him, she picked up his hand and cradled it between her own. She seemed to be mulling her words carefully, and he hated that, hated anyone treating him with kid gloves. He wasn't—

"Vincent's."

Her voice was a whisper, and they both flinched when she said it.

"I'm sorry. I know you loved something about him. I know that it's hard to separate what you loved from what he did to you. But he took my brother from me, and from everyone else who loved him. And now that we have you back? When you won't let people love you—" She turned her head away and wiped at her eyes. "Fuck these hormones. You deserve to be loved. Don't push this guy away, okay?"

"It might be too late for that."

"Well, *I* love you. The rest of our family loves you. If this doesn't work out with Ryan, you are still loved."

"Kimmy—"

"Don't you 'Kimmy' me." She stood up. "Call your boyfriend and grovel. Then come give me a hand behind the bar."

Ryan pulled the Volvo into the garage, put it in park, cut the engine, and rubbed his eyes. Emotional and physical depletion were par for the course during tech week, but the voice mail notification on his phone wasn't helping. He'd gotten a texted apology from Trey earlier, which he'd blown off because he was still pissed. What were the chances this message was from anyone else? Sure enough, when he tapped the voicemail icon, *Trey Donovan*, and a timestamp from the middle of rehearsal appeared. He pressed Play and Trey's voice filled his ear.

"It's me. I know you're in rehearsal, but I need to apologize, so I'm doing it here, at least until I get a chance to say it in person. I'm sorry. I was joking, but it was a bad joke. Not only was it in incredibly poor taste considering why you came home this summer, it was also a joke about your vulnerabilities, and I never meant to hurt you like that. I'm so sorry. If you never speak to me again, that's about what I deserve. But I hope you'll forgive me."

He listened to it again. And again. Finally, he got out of the car and made his way inside, closing the garage door. Ali was asleep on the couch, one arm shoved under a pillow, the other resting on her belly. She looked absurdly young and sweet, and for a moment he watched her sleep and said a silent prayer of thanks that she'd gotten sober. Then he shook her gently.

"Ry?" She blinked awake and winced. "Shit, I didn't mean to fall asleep. Is West home?"

"Not yet. Is he coming in tonight?"

She nodded sleepily and yawned. "I was waiting up for you guys, but the baby makes me so sleepy." Rubbing absently at her belly, she smiled. "How was dress?"

"Hectic. But good. It seems like this is the last ever tech week though. Mason and Caro think they need to close the theater at the end of the season."

"Oh no! When you said they had financial problems, I didn't realize you meant closing."

"The worst part is they won't let me help them. They say it's too late. I'm not so sure about that, but I don't know how to convince them."

"That's so sad." Ali stood up and wrapped her arms around him. "I'm sorry, goober."

He squeezed her back. "Thanks. What a rotten day."

"Have you eaten? I made a stir-fry. Pepper steak and vegetables. There's leftovers in the fridge."

"I haven't, but I don't have much of an appetite, to be honest."

Ali frowned. "Come on, you need to eat." She towed him by one arm into the kitchen and pushed him down in a chair at the table. "Sit. You're exhausted. I'll heat it up for you."

"Thanks, baby."

"What else happened today?" she asked as she grabbed the leftovers out of the fridge.

"Besides the theater closing news?"

"Yeah."

"How can you tell there's more?"

She shook her head and stirred the leftovers before sticking them in the microwave. "Because I know you, and I always know when you have something you don't want to tell me."

That wasn't fair. "I tell you everything."

"That doesn't mean you want to tell. There's a difference. So what's up?" She pulled the steaming container from the microwave and plunked it down unceremoniously on the table in front of him, then handed him the fork she'd used to stir it.

"Thanks."

"You're evading." She gave him a pointed look.

"I got in a fight with Trey. I think . . ." He shrugged and picked at his food.

"You're not sure?"

"Oh, I'm sure we got in a fight. He was a dick. I stomped off. He apologized. Twice. Now I—I don't know."

"You're still mad."

"No, I'm *not* mad." He shook his head and took a bite of the stir-fry. It seemed to stick in his throat when he tried to swallow, and he had to wash it down with a big gulp of water. "I'm hurt."

"Awww, honey." Ali rubbed his arm. "I'm sorry."

"Thanks. I don't know what to do. It scares me that he's able to hurt me like that."

"Yeah. That's the *worst* part about loving someone."

The buzzer for the gate sounded, and they looked at each other. Ali scrunched up her nose. "Well. Time to face the music."

Dusting off her hands on her jeans, she stood and crossed to the security panel to buzz the car service through the gate. She made a shooing gesture with her hands, and he took the hint. He put his uneaten food away—he didn't need another "this is how we get ants" lecture—and went upstairs to give her and West their privacy.

It was hours later and Ryan was dozing when someone knocked on his bedroom door. He sat up in bed and glanced at his phone: 1 a.m.

"Come on in."

West poked his head in. "I'm sorry, the light was on. I didn't realize you were asleep."

"Yeah, I fell asleep reading. Don't just stand there, come on in. Your flight went okay?"

West grinned and came over to sit at the foot of the bed. "I'm sure it was fine, but I was too goddamned nervous to do anything but bite my fingernails."

Pulling his legs up and wrapping his arms around his knees, Ryan made as much room as possible for West. "Are you a nervous flier?"

"No." West gave a short, brittle laugh. "I was nervous about all this. Ali—what if she didn't love me sober?"

"Ali loves you right down to the color of your snot," Ryan scoffed. "Gross."

"You're going to be someone's dad. There's a *lot* of snot in your future."

"And then there's that. I'm nervous about becoming a father. This is . . . unexpected. It's going to take some getting used to."

Ryan swallowed hard, then nodded. He couldn't imagine. Didn't want to imagine. He loved kids, but he still felt like one himself sometimes. Even the idea of taking care of a dog like Ferdy scared him. "Ali seems happy about it."

"Yeah." The smile that broke out across West's face rivaled a sunrise over the Atlantic in brilliance, but it faded just as fast. "So, there's no good way to ask this, but how long have you known?"

"Only since she got here, to Banker's Shoals."

"I understand why she kept it a secret." West blew out a breath and shook his head. "But I'm angry. And I'm terrified. And I'm furious that I'm terrified. But I love her—and oh shit, this is really fucking happening, isn't it?"

"You don't look terrified. For what it's worth."

"I'm a good actor."

Ryan smirked. "Eh, you're all right."

"Asshole."

"So listen, Trey walks his dog insanely early and I want to try to catch him in the morning. So if you and Ali need some more privacy, I can clear out for the day. No big."

"Trey—the boyfriend you've told me absolutely nothing about? The slut-shamer?"

Ryan blinked. *What the hell?* Then he remembered the conversation in the Ferrari.

"Ah, it's not like that. He's not a slut-shamer—at least not on purpose. That was a miscommunication."

"Ali likes him a lot."

Ryan smiled. He loved that Ali liked Trey. Loved that she understood how he made Ryan feel—both when he was happy and when he was hurt. "Yeah. He's the kind of guy who just makes you appreciate everything beautiful in life. And he's smoking hot."

"Yeah, Ali said so too." West flashed him a dirty smile and raised an eyebrow. "When do I get to meet him?"

"Never, you pervert." Ryan tossed a pillow at West's melodramatic pout, suddenly giddy and grateful to have his friends here in Banker's Shoals with him.

"Come on, Ryan. Introduce me to your boyfriend. I need to make sure he's good enough for you."

"But stay the fuck away from Trey Donovan. He's too good for you." Ryan flinched. But Mason had been *wrong*.

"He's good enough—and we're good *together*. I've never felt like this before. He said we're going to leave each other better than we found each other. But he makes me not want to leave at all."

West whistled. "Sounds pretty amazing, bro. How come you're sleeping alone?"

"I don't plan on this being permanent. We had a fight, but I'm going to fix it first thing tomorrow morning."

"Good. And then maybe invite him to brunch this weekend. Ali likes him, and for as long as I can, I want to make Ali happy."

"Thank god. Are y'all back together for good now?"

Smiling, West nodded. "We are. Ali changed her Facebook status from 'It's complicated' to 'In a relationship,' so it's even Facebook official."

"Well, if it's Facebook official . . ." Ryan cackled, then sobered. "Be patient with her—she's still working through a lot. But she loves you and the baby more than she wants to get high. I *know* this."

"I love her too. We're making plans—we'll be here in Banker's Shoals through opening night, then we're going to get her the best prenatal care money can buy in Los Angeles."

"Good." Ryan yawned and stretched. "Okay, dude, I gotta kick you out of my room now, because I have to get up early, and I'm *not* on California time."

"All right, I can take a hint. Good night." West ruffled Ryan's hair. "Thanks for taking care of Ali. I'm glad she has you."

Chapter Nineteen

Ryan's alarm went off at five thirty, and he almost hit the snooze button. But just because he didn't have dress rehearsal until that evening didn't mean he had nowhere to be. And he couldn't really hide from this conversation anymore. For about the eight millionth time, he brought up voice mail and listened to the message Trey had left the night before.

Lying in bed, Ryan felt claustrophobic and panicky—like he did while waiting in the wings before stepping out on stage on opening nights. Had he blown everything by falling asleep before calling Trey back? Trey's message had made it clear that he wanted to make up. But sometimes things looked different in the light of a new day. And Ryan hadn't called him back that night.

Just like there was nothing to be done about stage fright, there was nothing to be done about these nerves either—except facing them down. He rushed through his morning grooming routine, skipped the coffee altogether, and headed out for the beach with a baseball cap pulled over his hair and sunglasses hiding his eyes. He hoped this time he wouldn't be recognized by anyone.

Except maybe Ferdy.

He'd gone at least a half mile past where he usually ran into Trey, before the dog's distinctive bellow called from behind him. He turned around to see Ferdy dragging Trey along the beach.

"Let him go!" he shouted, surprising himself. Trey grinned and unclipped Ferdy's leash.

When was he going to get used to the sight of Ferdy hauling ass toward him, jowls flapping like wings, tail wagging like a propeller? This creature could probably take flight if he got going fast enough.

And yet somehow, he managed to stop just short of Ryan and crouch into a bow.

"Hey boy, hi Ferdy." Ryan bent down to scratch the soft ears that seemed too small for the giant head. Ferdy snorted, sighed, and knocked Ryan flat on his ass.

"Hi."

Ryan looked up at Trey and smiled. "Hi."

"I'm sorry I was a giant dick." Trey reached a hand down to Ryan to help him stand.

"I know you are. And I appreciate the apology. I listened to it about eleven billion times last night."

"I didn't want to call again because you've been super busy. You got a minute to talk now?"

"Call's not until six tonight. I've got all the time in the world."

"Okay. So we'll do this here?"

Laughter bubbled up out of Ryan. "As long as 'this' isn't going to get us arrested, sure."

"I realized I'd fucked up before the words were even out of my mouth. It was a bad, stupid, tasteless joke. I'm sorry I said it, not because I got the consequences I deserved, but because it hurt you, and I don't want to hurt you."

"Thank you. I accept your apology." Ryan smiled. "And I'm sorry I didn't call you back last night. I wanted to, but I fell asleep."

"No, that's fine. My therapist and my sister both think I was sabotaging our relationship because I'm still ashamed of what Vincent did to me." Trey squinted off at the horizon. "They're probably right."

Ryan's heart felt like it was going to break. "You don't have anything to be ashamed of. You have to know that."

Trey nodded, frowning still. "Knowing something intellectually and really *knowing* it all the way to your bones are two different things. It's a process—like learning a script."

"If you need someone to remind you, I'm here for that."

"What if I need someone to love me in spite of the way I put my foot in it when I'm scared? You got enough forgiveness?"

And just like that, there was a lump in Ryan's throat and he was nodding, and then they were kissing. His hat fell off, and he made a grab for it before laughing *and* crying into the kiss.

He didn't need the damned hat. Though he'd worn it out of habit, for all intents and purposes, he was *out* already, and he could kiss Trey on this empty beach and it wasn't *newsworthy* anymore.

He was free.

Yeah, he still had to sort out his career—but his personal life? That was as golden as a Carolina sunrise.

Ferdy nudged between them, and they broke apart, laughing.

Trey tucked a wayward strand of hair behind Ryan's ear, then picked up the baseball cap and eased it back onto Ryan's head with an affectionate tug on the brim. "I know you're living in the lap of luxury over at West's place, and I understand if this isn't something you'd like, but I would love it if you would maybe come spend some nights at my place too? We could watch old movies and cook tacos and have lots of really super amazing sex. Make the most of the time you've got left here."

"'Really super amazing'? How much time have you been spending with Ali?"

Trey scowled playfully. "One car drive and 'really super' has become an enduring part of my vocabulary. So, what do you say? Come hang out after dress tonight and maybe stay?"

That was easy. "Yes."

"One word, and you knock the breath out of me." Trey drew him into another kiss—one that hinted at things they would absolutely get arrested for doing on a public beach.

"Hmmm, save that for later," Ryan murmured, laughing.

"Whenever you want."

"This is Ali Parker's house?" Kim stared, wide-eyed, at West's house as they pulled through the gate and approached the front. Ali had invited them for brunch—a perfect opportunity to introduce the two women.

"Ish." Trey smiled at his starstruck sister. "Technically West Brady's house, but they're together."

"Look at you, knowing more celebrity gossip than *People* magazine."

"I guess that comes from dating a TV star." Trey scrunched up his face. "I honestly don't know how that happened."

Kim laughed. "I do. He walked into the bar and you couldn't take your eyes off him. And apparently, he has excellent taste."

Trey cut a side-eye at her and then walked around the truck to help her. As she stepped down, she winced and put a hand under her belly, taking a deep breath. Alarm shot through him.

"Are you okay?"

"I'm fine." She rolled her eyes. "Having another human being moving around inside your body sometimes squishes things that shouldn't be squished. Like your bladder. Or your sciatic nerve. Or your lungs. Or your stomach. Or your—"

"Uncle." He held up both hands. "I believe you."

"Don't ask a pregnant woman if she's okay unless you want to know."

"Lesson learned."

"Man, it stinks Danny is missing this." She stared wistfully up at the house. "That front porch would give him ideas."

Danny had been called down to Savannah to the first bar he and Kim had opened together, when their manager had unexpectedly quit earlier that week.

"Somehow I doubt this is the last chance he'll have to meet them. Come on, I'll introduce you to Ali." He held out a hand to steady her over the sandy driveway, and she rolled her eyes again but let him take her arm.

Ryan opened the door with a huge grin and moved in to kiss Trey—a quick hello with a smaller, intimate smile and a brief caress to his face. For a moment, Trey's world was filled with nothing but Ryan—the clean smell of his body, the brush of fingers, the soft press of lips and the barest touch of tongue. He wanted to forget about brunch, drag Ryan upstairs, and kiss him until they were both hard and gasping.

He wanted more time.

Ryan pulled away with a searching look, but whatever he saw in Trey's eyes just made his face go soft as he let go of Trey.

He turned and took Kim's arm. "Hi, Kim. It's nice to see you again. You make a mean margarita—so if I don't seem to remember much of our first meeting, please take it as a compliment to your bartending skills, and not, you know, personal. Now, let me introduce you to my best friend in the world—she's been dying to meet you. And she's put out an incredible spread."

Trey trailed into the kitchen after them, watching Ryan charm his sister, who laughed and blushed at the attention from an honest-to-god Hollywood star.

Ali and Kim hit it off immediately, their excited chatter filling the kitchen. Ryan hadn't been kidding—Ali truly had put out an incredible spread. The countertop island had been transformed to a magazine-worthy buffet—bagels with smoked salmon and capers, coddled eggs in tiny cups, enough fresh fruit to feed a dozen people, and beautifully folded, airy crepes, with small bowls of various fillings.

"Wow—Ali, this is amazing."

"I didn't make the bagels—there's a little place on Main Street owned by a guy who moved down from New York. But thank you." She came over and gave him a hug. "Have you met West yet?"

An impeccably styled man with black curly hair and bright-blue eyes stepped forward with his hand extended. Trey clasped it and let himself be pulled into a brotherly embrace. West was handsome in that old-school Hollywood way. More polished and reserved on first glance than Ryan or Ali, but when he smiled, pure mischief filled his eyes. "It's nice to meet the man who tamed Bryan Hart."

Trey started to stammer out an answer, uncomfortably aware of how attractive West was and how out of place he felt in the man's presence. Whereas Ryan—in his hippie sandals and frat-bro baseball caps—was comfortably, approachably handsome, West was . . . something else.

Ryan cackled and slung an arm over Trey's shoulder, whispering theatrically, "Don't mind him, he's too pretty for his own good, and he *knows* the effect he has on people."

"It's nice to meet you too," Trey mumbled, blushing.

Taking West's hand, Ali beamed, and the man's smile went soft and smitten when he looked down at her, not intimidating at all.

"Welcome to our home, Trey. Kim." West gestured around him. "And thank you for joining us for brunch. It's wonderful to be surrounded by friends on a Sunday morning. I'm not a religious man, so I don't say grace, but I want to say that I'm thankful to have you all here."

"Amen," Ryan said enthusiastically, earning himself an exasperated glance from West. "Let's eat, yeah?"

"Yes, please. I'm starving." Ali started passing out plates. "Help yourselves, guys. There's fresh-squeezed orange juice in the fridge, regular and decaf coffee on the counter."

Conversation over the table ranged from pregnancy—in detail Trey had no desire to know about but somehow became fascinated by—to the inevitable discussion of Shakespeare by the Sea and the decision to close after the season.

"I wish they would let me help." Ryan frowned, and Trey took his hand under the table. "But Mason won't take money from me."

"Maybe you can find a way to help without offering money," Ali suggested.

"I'm already working for free. That's a big deal. If I know Mason, he's probably paying the other actors more than he would if I weren't doing this pro bono, but there's nothing I can do about that."

West steepled his fingers together under his chin, apparently lost in thought until he asked, "What exactly is the problem?"

"Ticket sales are down," Trey answered for Ryan. "They draw up the budget based on seating seventy-five percent of the house for each show, ad revenues, and local arts endowments."

"Right. That sounds pretty typical. I'm guessing the crew is mostly local and nonunion?"

"Correct." Ryan cocked his head to one side. "You're not suggesting they cut crew?"

"No." West waved a hand. "No, I'm not. It's good, from a sheer cash flow standpoint, that they can get nonunion labor, however—no offense, Trey—"

"None taken—yet." He just loved how the words *no offense* typically preceded something offensive.

"—They would have more predictable, if higher, costs using union stagehands."

"I don't know that predictability in costs is a problem," Ryan mused. "I could be wrong, but I think costs tend to be fairly stable."

"But they aren't getting the word out to enough theatergoers to get butts in seats, even with a famous star?"

"They aren't using his name in the advertising," Trey pointed out. "So no one knows."

"Well, that's—"

"Bullshit, is what it is," Ryan interrupted West with a scowl. "Mason's bullshit pride."

"That's not true. It was Caro's decision." Trey couldn't let this be another bone of contention between Ryan and Mason, not when he knew the truth.

Ryan's mouth fell open. "Caro?"

"Yeah, something about your privacy—but also about your reputation. She doesn't want to exploit you."

"*Exploit* me? How the hell is advertising my presence here *exploiting* me?"

"It sounds to me," Ali spoke up, "that you need to take the decision out of their hands."

Everyone turned their attention to Ali, who shrugged. "It's Ryan's privacy, right? And Ryan's reputation. It seems to me that despite Caro's best efforts, you've still been photographed naked, outed on the internet, and speculated to be my baby's daddy."

"So what have I got to lose?" Ryan grinned. "I like it."

"Like what?" Trey looked between Ryan and Ali, who were exchanging conspiratorial smiles. "What are you up to?"

"I'm going to save my cousin's theater. But I can't do it alone. All by myself, I'm not a big enough story."

"And that's where West and I come in," Ali added.

"Me? What do I have to do with it?" West looked as baffled as Trey felt.

Ryan turned to West, hands waving animatedly. "How do you feel about doing an exclusive interview about the three of us? Our friendship, the baby coming. You guys coming here to support me doing a season of summer stock?"

"Oh, I see where you're going with this. Get the news out on the internet now—dropped in the middle of a bigger human-interest story, and people will be scrambling for tickets. I'm in. Anything you need."

"Who can we get to do the interview?" Ali mused. "Barbara Walters won't even look at me until I've been clean longer than a few weeks."

"Too old-school anyway." West shook his head. "A prime-time special needs to be recorded and booked out way in advance. You don't want TV. You *need* clickbait."

"The *BS Herald*'s website couldn't handle the traffic if this is as big as we want it to be." Ryan scowled. "I hate to say it, but—"

"No." Ali shook her head. "Ryan, no."

"You guys are freaking me out with this psychic link shit," Kim said.

"Come on, Ali. They're already here. I might even recognize the guy if I see him." Ryan turned to Trey. "There are going to be questions about you. Are you comfortable being referred to as my boyfriend?"

Trey's heart felt like it was going to flutter out of his chest. "I— Of course. Are you?"

Ryan leaned in and kissed him, hard, right there at the table. "Yes."

"In *Gossip Miner*, Ryan?" Ali's voice went shrill.

"Oh, hell yes." Ryan grinned. "I'm not letting your 'bisexual baby' get more clicks than me."

"Mike is going to kill you." Ali rubbed her belly and scowled. "If I don't kill you first. It's the principle of the thing."

Sobering up at the mention of his agent's name, Ryan frowned. "If Mike can't get work for an out bisexual actor, he probably shouldn't be working in Hollywood. And *he* works for *me*."

Pumping his fist in the air, West practically roared. "*Yes*, he does. And it's about damned time you learned that."

Ali shot West a withering glare. "Easy for you to say, you're Hollywood royalty."

"And you and Ryan are my family." West grinned. "He's finally figured out who works for who. He pays Mike, not the other way around." He turned to Ryan. "I'm proud of you, brother. Let's make this happen."

Chapter Twenty

Ryan helped West clean up the kitchen while Ali and Kim pored over baby furniture on their phones, occasionally asking Trey's opinion on construction options and styles. They all huddled together on the sofa, two red heads and one brown; Ryan couldn't stop smiling at the sight.

"I like him," West said. "He seems like a steady, upstanding guy. Cute too."

"He is, isn't he?" Trey might not think of himself as cute, but Ryan had a hard time keeping his eyes off the man who had eased into his heart. "I'm crazy about him."

West bumped their shoulders together. "I'm glad you found someone."

With hardly any persuading at all, Ryan decided to go home with Trey for the night, so he said his good-byes to West and Ali, and climbed into the backseat of Trey's truck.

"Thank you for letting me ride shotgun." Kim glanced over her shoulder at him as she buckled her seat belt. "And thank you both for introducing me to Ali—she's wonderful. It's so nice to have another woman nearby who's in the same stage of pregnancy as I am."

The sweet smile Trey turned to his sister made Ryan's heart thump heavier in his chest. God, he was falling hard. He was so caught up in fantasies about how he'd spend the afternoon and evening with Trey, he almost didn't notice the red Toyota idling a few hundred yards down the street.

The same red Toyota he frequently saw parked in that exact spot down the street from West's front gate. The same red Toyota that frequently parked in the public beach spots while he was in rehearsal.

"Stop, stop the car!"

Trey slammed on the brakes. "What is it?"

"I'll tell you in a minute."

Jumping out of the truck, Ryan pulled up the *Gossip Miner* article on his phone, then marched over to the car and rapped on the window with his knuckles. The driver lowered it, looking sheepish.

"Can I help you?"

"Did you take this picture?" Ryan pointed at the photo of him and Trey kissing.

"Yeah, so what? I was on a public street, it's not a crime to photograph someone in public."

"I'm not mad about the picture. You work for *Gossip Miner*?"

"I'm freelance."

"Yeah? Can you write?"

"Of course. I'm a journalist."

"Journalist my ass," Ryan scoffed. "Right now, you're garbage. You go around trying to catch people in compromising positions so you can embarrass them for profit. But if you can write? If you're any good at it? I can *make* you a journalist." Ryan shoved his phone back in his pocket. "How would you like an exclusive interview with me, West Brady, and Ali Parker?"

"For serious?"

"If you can write—and I will be checking up on you—then we'll go on the record about why I'm here, about Ali's pregnancy, about my sexuality even."

"Hell yeah. If you go on the record—I could sell that anywhere."

"Give me your card."

The guy scrambled around in the glove box, fumbling with a card case and finally depositing a business card in Ryan's hand. "Geoff Walsh. I've mostly done sports writing. The photography is a side hobby. Then when I found out you were in town—you know that picture in the *Herald*?"

The one of his ass. "Yeah, I know the one."

"I heard they paid that kid two hundred and fifty bucks for the photo—and he took that on an iPhone. It seemed like getting some better shots and selling them to bigger publications could be good money." He shrugged. "It's not illegal."

"We've established that." As much as he hated rewarding this slimeball's behavior, he didn't have a lot of time—and this guy already had contacts at *Gossip Miner*. Ryan gestured with the card. "I'm going to read your work. If I like what I see, I'll call you tomorrow."

"I'm just trying to make a living, man."

"Yeah, me too." Ryan turned and walked back to Trey's truck. When he got in, Trey and Kim both stared at him, eyes wide.

"What was that all about?" Kim asked.

"We might have a 'journalist'—" he made scare quotes around the word "—to help us save the theater."

"The guy who's been stalking you? Ryan—"

Ryan held up his hands. "I know, it sounds crazy—but he's here now. He doesn't have to charter a flight. He already has connections with the gossip sites. He can provide exactly the sort of sleazy gossip-driven clickbait we need. It's perfect."

"I'll take your word for it." Trey put the truck back in gear. "I hope this plan of yours works."

"Me too."

Chapter Twenty-One

Geoff Walsh, it turned out, *could* write. He'd been covering local sports—mostly high school, but some college games too—for the past five years. A lot of his pieces were the kind of hokey human interest stories the athletes' mothers would keep in a scrapbook, but his writing was clean, careful, and emotive without being over the top. It was humanizing.

After clearing it with Ali and West, Ryan scheduled the interview.

Walsh was obviously nervous when he arrived at the beach house. He held up his camera. "I've gotten some interest already, but they want photos. Is that okay?"

"How nice of you to ask," Ali murmured drily.

West sat down next to her and took her hand, while Ryan sat on her other side and wished like hell Trey were there to hold *his* hand, because his nerves felt like opening night without the anticipation. What if this plan didn't work? What if, for all his "he works for me" bravado, he got blowback from his agent, and it didn't even help the theater? What if—

"Breathe, goober." Ali poked him in the ribs. "It's going to be okay."

Walsh held up his digital recorder.

"Shall we get started?"

Trey watched from the couch as a shirtless Ryan paced around the living room with his phone, nervous as a cat in a room full of rocking chairs. Every time Ryan paced close to Ferdy's mattress, the big dog would cock his head to the side. Finally, Ryan flopped down next to Ferdy, buried his face on the dog's shoulder, and let out a muffled groan.

"Waiting is killing me."

Ferdy snuffled his head, then licked his hair. Trey stifled a laugh as Ryan sat back up with a shout.

"That's what you get for going to a mastiff for comfort instead of your boyfriend who happens to be sitting right freaking here."

Ryan looked at the dog, then back at Trey. "I'm sorry, did I hurt your feelings?"

"My feelings are fine. If you're *up* for it, I know how to take your mind off the wait." Trey palmed himself through his jeans. "Come here."

Those fey hazel eyes of Ryan's widened, and his Adam's apple bobbed in his throat as he swallowed. "There?"

Trey nodded, and Ryan stood up and crossed the room. Even though it was warm in the house, goose bumps were scattered across Ryan's naked chest. As soon as he was in arm's reach, Trey gripped him around the waist and pulled him close so he could trace them with his tongue.

"Oh my god," Ryan murmured, his head falling back.

Would Trey ever get enough of how Ryan felt under his hands? He ran them up over Ryan's nipples, trying to memorize the gasps and the shivers of Ryan's response. Touching Ryan might as well be catching lightning in a mason jar—no matter how electric it was, it couldn't last forever. Every laughter-filled kiss was one kiss closer to the end of summer, and Ryan's return to LA. Trey shuddered, and his hands tightened on Ryan's hips. To hide the sudden melancholy sweeping through him, he leaned down and tugged the button of Ryan's shorts open with his teeth.

Ryan's hand came to rest on Trey's head as he eased the zipper open and tugged Ryan's briefs and shorts down to expose his cock. Trey took his time worshipping Ryan's dick, rubbing his lips along the length and tugging gently on the sack. As much as he wanted to take Ryan deep and hear him groan, he held off. He licked lightly at the head, then drew back and blew on the tender skin.

"Oh— Fuck that's— You're a goddamn tease." Ryan groaned.

"Mmm." Trey hummed and gave Ryan's balls another tug. "What do you want, Ryan? You want me to fuck you?"

"I want your mouth on my dick."

Trey smiled up at him wickedly, then gave him another slow swipe of his tongue. "Seems like you've already got that."

Ryan jerked at his hair. "Please?"

And Trey couldn't resist that request. He took as much of Ryan into his mouth as he could, pulling back only when his eyes watered and he gagged. Ryan's hips moved forward, as if chasing Trey's mouth.

"I can't—" Ryan grasped Trey's hair with both hands, like he was trying to gain control of his own body through holding on to Trey. But that wasn't what Trey wanted. He wanted Ryan out of control like the summer storm he was. He pulled off Ryan's dick and looked him right in the eyes.

"Don't hold back."

Before Ryan could say anything more, Trey took him deep again. Was he trying to prove something to Ryan? To himself? Did it matter when Ryan was groaning like that, and burying his hands in Trey's hair? Trey let go of Ryan's hips and let Ryan take over the pace, let him push deeper and drive in harder.

Letting someone else take control like this, use him like this— this was a measure of trust he hadn't given anyone in a long time, and it was decadent and thrilling and terrifying all at once.

He gagged again, and tears sprang into his eyes, but then Ryan bit out a whispered, "I'm gonna—"

Trey grabbed Ryan's hips and swallowed around him, letting him know this wasn't just okay, this was what he wanted—

"Oh, I love—love—ahh—" Ryan babbled and came, and Trey did his best to swallow it all.

Ryan collapsed down next to him on the couch, kissing his shoulder, then his chest, then straddling his lap and kissing him hard, like he didn't care that he'd just fucked Trey's face and come in his mouth.

Like he didn't realize he'd almost said, *I love you.*

Trey kissed him back, clumsy and shaking. Somehow the blowjob intended to distract Ryan had turned *Trey* inside out instead.

Then Ryan was on his knees, pulling at Trey's cutoff sweatpants and *holy shit* his hands felt good, and his mouth, desperate, eager, and hot—

"Fuck!" Trey's already-on-edge body rushed past the clouds-rolling-in stage and right onto storm surge. "Ry, I'm gonna come."

Ryan's eyes met his, and he somehow managed to flash a grin—or the idea of one—around Trey's cock, and that was all it took for the overwhelming pleasure to course through his body. Ryan's hands and mouth gentled, and he rose up over Trey to kiss him again, long and sweet. When he moved away, he stared Trey in the eye and smiled.

"I love you. I'm sorry to be that cliché of a guy who says it in bed. But I wanted you to know."

Trey's heart pounded in his chest as he stared back at Ryan. Finally he said, "Technically, we're on the sofa."

Ryan grinned and reached for his clothes, but then dropped them and kissed Trey again until they were both stretched out, skin to skin, the heat rising between them.

Ryan's phone beeped, and they broke apart, breathing hard. Ryan gave Trey an apologetic shrug, then fished it out of his shorts and glanced at the screen.

His eyes met Trey's.

"It's live."

Trey shook a heavy set piece with all his strength, testing to expose any last-minute vulnerabilities. While he trusted the stagehands to move and reattach the set pieces properly, this was his first time designing a set on wheels—and he'd be damned if he was going to let the show go on without regular examination of the hardware.

"It's fine." Caro rolled her eyes. "I've got the hands looking over all the joins every time they move the pieces. We'll know if there's trouble before it's a thing."

"It's dark on stage. Humor me and let me inspect it myself."

"All right." She shrugged. "We trust you, though."

"Caroline Evelyn Hertzog!" Mason's voice boomed through the theater. Trey's eyes met Caro's.

"Did he just middle-name you?"

"As bad as my mother." She grimaced, then shouted back: "What'd I do?"

Mason stormed out of the wings onto the stage. "Your cousin."

"Ryan?" Trey glanced at Caro. "What'd *he* do?"

"He gave a fucking interview to *Gossip Miner* is what he did." Mason thrust his phone into Caro's hands. "And our box office phone hasn't stopped ringing for the last hour—I've been covering the overflow of calls for Tabitha."

Letting out a whoop, Trey picked up Caro and swung her around. "It fucking worked, didn't it?"

"You *knew* about this?" Mason growled.

"Dude, you're big and scary, but have you met my dog?" Trey patted Mason's arm. "Yeah, I was with him and Ali and West when they came up with the idea."

"Holy shit, he came *out*." Caro was scanning the website, wide-eyed. "Aww, Trey."

"Okay, skip that part." Trey grinned. "You guys don't have to worry about his reputation. He makes his own choices, and he's doing Hollywood on his own terms."

The box office door sprang open and Tabitha, the head of ticket sales, emerged with a shocked expression on her face.

"We sold out. Opening weekend is sold out. Both nights, both matinees."

"I gotta call Ryan," Caro practically squealed.

"What does this mean?" Trey grabbed Mason's arm. "Is it—is it enough?"

Mason put his hand over Trey's, gently detangling them. "I don't know. Goddamn. I don't know. But that man of yours is something, isn't he?"

Trey grinned. "Yeah he is."

Chapter Twenty-Two

Ryan arrived at the theater two hours before call for opening night, and cornered Caro and Mason in the office.

"If it's not too late—I spoke to my lawyer and my accountant, and I want to create an endowment for the theater so you guys don't find yourself counting pennies at the start of every season. It won't solve all your financial problems, but it will help. Can we do this?"

Caro glanced at Mason, and the two of them seemed to share some silent communication. Finally, she sighed and turned back to Ryan.

"It feels wrong taking your money. But yes, we can."

"Why does it feel wrong? You have at least two other endowments that I know of. And I'm not even asking for advertising in exchange. I only want to help."

"I'm sorry, Ryan. I still think of you as my little cousin who I have to take care of. With the shoe on the other foot—I guess it's hard for me to accept."

Mason looked down at the desk, then at Caro, then back to Ryan. "After your interview went up on that gossip site, we sold out this weekend's performances—and ticket sales are up for the whole season."

"I thought that might happen." Ryan smiled. "I still don't understand your reluctance. Isn't that why you hired me? 'Cause I'm famous and working for free?"

"We hired you because you're a talented actor who shows up on time to work and was willing to work for free," Caro answered. "We didn't exploit your name—shut up, Mason—we didn't exploit your name because you needed time away from all the Hollywood bullshit.

How would it have helped you to have the Hollywood bullshit follow you home?"

"How would it have helped me to have home no longer be here because you two were too stubborn to let me help?"

They didn't have an answer for that.

"I love you guys for letting me come home and figure my shit out. And, Mason, I love you for letting me be a cast member in this amazing, talented company. You're the best Shakespearean actor I know, and this theater is a treasure."

Mason smiled. "Thank you, Ryan. I'm glad to have you in my company. For all my reservations at the beginning, I'm proud of you—not just on stage." Mason shifted from one foot to the other, obviously uncomfortable.

Blushing, Ryan ducked his head. All he'd ever wanted was this kind of praise from Mason, and now he found himself tongue-tied. "I'm just doing my job."

"And you're doing it well." Caro squeezed him around the waist. "Thank you for being here this summer."

"You're welcome. Now, I'm going to go for a walk to clear my head, and I'll see you guys soon."

He made his way down to the ghost-lit stage and climbed the steps to the little balcony he and Trey had painted. Stretching out on his back and studying the ceiling, he let the turmoil of his thoughts rumble around each other. The man he loved would be in the audience tonight, watching him perform to a sold-out crowd. Against all odds, he'd managed to help save the theater and maybe his reputation too. So why did it feel like everything was ending instead of beginning?

A noise from below caught his attention, and he sat up. Annsley was walking in a circle around the stage.

"Hey," he called out, and she looked up and waved.

"Hi. What're you doing up there?"

He shrugged. "Opening night melancholy. You?"

"Something like that." She crossed the stage and climbed the steps to sit with him. "So, um. We all read the interview. It was really good."

"Yeah? It seems to have done the trick. We're sold out for the weekend."

"Yeah. Let's see, what was my favorite part?" She pantomimed concentrating then, "Oh! I think it was 'Hart describes his bisexuality in frank, no-nonsense terms, but when asked about his current relationship status, he blushes like a teenaged virgin and admits there is someone very special.'"

"Oh god." Ryan buried his reddening face in his palms. "It sounds so cheesy when you say it like that." The article had gone on to profile Trey in breathless—but shallow—speculation.

"It's sweet. Trey's a lucky guy." She leaned against him, pressing their arms together. "Thank you for everything you've done for me this summer."

He slung an arm around her shoulders and squeezed. "It's an honor to share the stage with you. You're going to be an incredible Beatrice."

"Thank you. You've been an incredible mentor."

Remembering the dressing down he'd taken from her earlier over their scandal earlier that summer, he smiled. "So have you, Ann."

She sniffled, laughed, and punched his arm. "I'm about to cry, so I'd better head back to the house to get some carbs in me before the show. The rest of the cast is there too—want to come?"

"Nah. I'm just going to sit here for a while. Calm before the storm, you know?" He shrugged. He'd grown to enjoy his castmates' company, but on opening night, he prized his solitude.

"Okay. See you in a couple hours." Annsley gave him a last hug good-bye, then hurried off, wiping her eyes.

Opening nights were emotional for everyone, but for Ryan, this night was the culmination not only of weeks of rehearsals, but also his efforts to figure out who he was beyond "the party guy."

He was Mark Antony, and Don Pedro, and Bryan Hart.

And he was Ryan Hertzog—a bisexual actor from North Carolina who had finally found comfort in his own skin.

I only hope my career survives.

The energy in the dressing room backstage was intense—nervous and animated as everyone tugged on their tunics, togas, and sandals.

Julius Caesar was a tragedy, and the actors' faces were grim with concentration and tight with focus as they ran through their favorite vocal warm-ups.

"How's it going, David?" Ryan took an empty seat at the vanity beside the Brutus to his Antony, and met his eyes in the mirror.

David was still green from his bout with food poisoning over two weeks before—he'd only barely made it out of the hospital in time for dress last week. The bright dressing room lights emphasized his pallor.

"Fucking salmonella," he moaned. "I have the worst UTI."

Oh, *ouch*. "Are you going to be okay?"

David shuddered. "The show must go on, right?"

Ryan gave his shoulder a squeeze. "Yeah, buddy. Can I get you anything?"

"Can you pop into the girls' dressing room and ask Ann to come over with my pills? I forgot to take them out of her purse when we got here."

"Sure."

Though the theater had been built with two dressing rooms out of some sense of propriety, theater folk were known for their lack of giving a shit about propriety. Men and women walked in and out of both dressing rooms with no one batting an eyelash. Ryan found Annsley applying makeup at the vanity.

"Hey, gorgeous." He sat next to her.

"Hey, Ry. Or are we calling you Bryan now that your secret is out? I can't keep track."

"Whatever you want. So, David is . . . not good."

She put down her eyeliner and pointed to the cubby holding her street clothes. "I don't know which pill he needs for whatever particular not-good he's feeling but there's a whole arsenal of them in my bag. Just take the whole thing to him, and make him drink a bottle of water."

"Yes, ma'am." He grabbed her handbag and blew her a kiss. "Break a leg, Ann."

"You too, Hertzog." She stuck her tongue out at him in the mirror and then went back to her face.

In the men's dressing room, he handed David the purse.

"Bless you," David said gratefully. Ryan nodded and went to find Caro. No surprise, she was in the lighting booth with Viki, making sure everything was working correctly before they opened the theater to guests.

"Hey, Caro, you still keep a stash of bottled water in the office fridge?"

She looked up. "Yeah. For David?"

"The show must go on." He shrugged.

At seven thirty, the lights went down over the house and came up on stage. The actors and crew watched in silence as Mason walked out to the center of the stage in an honest-to-god tuxedo to address the crowd.

"Shakespeare by the Sea is a Banker's Shoals summer tradition. Tonight, we welcome you to opening night of the 2017 summer stock season with our production of *Julius Caesar*. Enjoy the show."

The show itself was Shakespeare at its very best: biting wit and timeless drama. David, for all his green face before the show, shone as the complicated Brutus. Ryan, who had practiced Antony's "Friends, Romans, countrymen" soliloquy in front of a mirror since he was twelve years old, played the part like an impression of his oldest, dearest friend.

And the sold-out audience roared.

Chapter Twenty-Three

Six weeks—a folly? An idyll? Shakespeare would have had a word for it.

Over the course of the season, Ryan fell into the rhythm of the production as he always did, with one exception. Giddy from the thrill of performing, the cast frequently moved on to the parties afterward. Ryan was happy to skip the parties—and the hangovers—and go home to Trey horny and ready to make more dirty memories to cherish when the summer came to an end.

And life with Trey over those six weeks was nothing short of perfect. Trey made his own schedule, often doing rental house maintenance, so he was busy, but able to swing by the house to have lunch—or sometimes a nooner—with Ryan. He came to as many of the shows as he could, until he could probably recite every line of both plays as easily as Ryan himself.

But six weeks came to an inevitable close, and Ryan woke up that last morning frowning and melancholy.

"You could stay here." Trey traced Ryan's lips with his finger as early-morning sunlight poured through the curtains of his bedroom. "West is going to want his house back, but you can live with me. And . . . I don't know. You're a partner in the theater now. You could be a real part of it."

Ryan nipped absently at Trey's finger. He wanted nothing more than to be cocooned in Trey's arms forever. He could be himself here in a way he'd forgotten how to be in California, where his job was tied up in keeping up appearances. Keeping up appearances wasn't who he was—he knew that now. But the job? The art? That *was* who he was. A defining part of him. And the ambition that propelled him across the country seven years earlier would never be satisfied if he didn't give it another try. He didn't want to end up resenting Trey for being the reason he gave up a dream he'd had since childhood.

"I can't stay." He saw the disappointment in Trey's face, and it killed him. "If I stay here now—it's like giving up on those dreams that sent me west in the first place. It's like saying all those people who thought I wasn't good enough, the ones who thought I was nothing but a party boy, a D-list nobody with a pretty face that wouldn't last long—it's saying those people were right. It's letting the gossip be true. And it's—it's letting a campy sci-fi show that was canceled halfway through the first season be my best work. And I'm not done, man. I'm only twenty-five. I've made some mistakes, but don't I deserve a chance to prove I'm more than my mistakes?"

"Of course you do." Shoving away from Ryan, Trey scrubbed a hand over his face. "Of course. I'm just being selfish."

"You could come with me. Mike got me a six-episode guest run on *Triage*. You could come out for a week or two and see Hollywood. I could take you to some of the studios."

Trey shook his head. "We're being silly now. Trying to turn our summer together into a life—that's not how it works. We both know better."

Ryan's chest was splitting in two. "I don't. I don't know better. I don't even know how this works. I know I have to leave, and I know I don't want to leave you."

"You're talking about putting a Band-Aid on an amputation."

"I'm talking about our life!"

"It's won't be temporary long distance. We're talking an entire continent between us for—for months at a time. What kind of life is that?"

"That's the life of a guy who works in movies," Ryan snapped. "You knew who I was. And you knew I was leaving." He stood up and started pacing around the room. "So this is how it ends? Us bitching at each other because you won't leave and I won't stay, and we're too damned stubborn to try and find a compromise?"

"What kind of compromise is there?"

"I could try to find work on the East Coast. New York—or Atlanta even. Atlanta's got a booming television and film industry. It's not a perfect solution, but it's something, right? Please don't make it be all or nothing." Ryan knelt by the bed and took Trey's hand between his own, pressing the knuckles to his lips. "Give me a chance to try to have it all."

"Now who's being selfish?" Trey squeezed Ryan's hand, letting him know he was teasing. "I don't know. A clean break is probably for the best, don't you think? I don't want to fall out of love by attrition. If we end it like this—at least we had one amazing summer together that we can look back on fondly."

Well, that was that. Bitterness washed over Ryan, who stood up and turned away to hide the wetness in his eyes.

"Okay, then. I guess I'd better pack. I've got to get to Dare County Airport by three. And if you won't even try, I don't have anything left to say."

"Ryan, don't be like that. Can we just do this like adults?"

Ryan yanked a T-shirt over his head. "That's the second time you've called me a child. The first time, I believed you when you said it was a joke. Now I think it's just your way of pretending what I want doesn't matter. And you know—I get that your ex did a number on you and you can't let yourself be vulnerable. I get it."

"This isn't about him."

"Isn't it?" Ryan gestured around the room. "Isn't every fight we've *ever* had at least a little bit about him? I'm not asking you to marry me. I'm asking you to spend a few weeks in California and let me share something of myself with you."

"Why?"

"Because I love you. And I don't think you want this to end either, but I need to start being Bryan Hart again—and if you can't love that part of me too? I'll see myself out."

Ryan started shoving clothes in his overnight bag. Shorts, T-shirt, *goddamn it*, where had his underwear gone? Blinking back tears at the sudden reminder of his first morning in this house, he dug his fist into his forehead and took a deep breath.

"You can keep the underwear."

"Ry—"

Ferdy's bark cut off the rest of his name as Ryan strode through the living room to the back door.

That was fine. By the time he landed on the West Coast that afternoon, he'd be Bryan Hart again.

Whoever that was.

Chapter Twenty-Four

Ryan set the script down on Mike's desk with shaking fingers. It was good. *Really* good. Academy Award good. And they wanted him. No audition necessary, they'd *specifically* asked for him. So why did he feel uneasy about it? Sure, he'd rather not spend six months shooting in Texas, of all places, but it was a good role—and it was a lead role. It could be the *perfect* role to make the leap from character actor to leading man. And the idea of taking it filled him with dread.

"As your agent, I should caution you—I don't know that playing a young gay man from the South is the best idea so soon after coming out," Mike said. "But your work since you've been back in town has caught the best kind of attention. You have your pick of 'young gay man' roles, and there's Emmy whispers for the work you did on *Triage*."

"Yeah, I'll believe that when I see it." Ryan shook his head. The popular hospital show had put him through the ringer in the role of a paramedic held hostage with the ER staff by a gunman and the whirlwind romance with a nurse that followed. It had been some of his best work—but award-worthy? No one with a brain in their head was going to give Ryan an award for anything.

"What the hell is wrong with you?" Mike's voice cut through the fog of misery Ryan had once again wrapped himself in.

Ryan looked up. "Nothing. I'm fine. You're probably right about the gay thing; I don't want to get type cast. But this is a great opportunity. How much time do I have to think it over?"

"I'll call the casting director and let them know you need a few days, but you're leaning toward yes. The dancing show called again. They offered—"

"No reality TV." Ryan cut him off. "They literally cannot pay me enough to do another reality show."

"Let me put out some more feelers. Jesus, you're one grumpy motherfucker. Do you think you can cheer the fuck up before your audition tomorrow?"

Oh yeah. The teenage drama needing a high school teacher. He was pleasantly surprised he hadn't been called to audition for the role of one of the kids, but slightly terrified that he was now too old to play a teenager on TV.

"No. I can't *cheer the fuck up*. But I'm an actor, so I'll act."

"Listen, Ryan, I know I was a dick last spring, but you've done incredible work since then. You should be proud of what you've accomplished over the last few months. And I can't believe I'm saying this, but if quitting drinking has made you miserable, do me a favor and go on a bender. Just stay out of the papers."

"I didn't quit drinking." Ryan looked down at the script on the desk again. "I mean, I guess I did—but it wasn't a conscious decision. Anyway, getting drunk isn't going to make me feel better. But I'll keep it in mind."

"What can I do? This is what we've been busting our asses for. You have everything you ever wanted."

No, I don't.

"What kind of role is going to make you happy?" Mike spread his hands wide. "You're in your *prime*. I just want to help you make it last."

"I don't know. I doubt playing a high school teacher is going to do the trick."

Mike gave a helpless shrug. "All right. Call me after, let me know how it goes."

"You're going to take root on that barstool." Kim glared at Trey across the bar. "Not that I don't enjoy your scintillating company, but you do realize that when I get home, I'm going to be up with a colicky baby every two hours. You're actually making me look forward to pacing around his bedroom."

"Whatever." Trey kept his eyes on the football game on the screen above the bar with halfhearted interest. But even men in tight pants grappling with each other didn't hold much appeal.

"Have you talked to Doc Wharton about your depression?"

"I'm not depressed."

"You haven't mentioned her lately. Have you been to see her?"

"No."

"Don't you think that's kind of important? Seeing as how you have posttraumatic stress disorder after your husband tried to kill you?"

"She hasn't done any more for me than you have."

"That is *bullshit*. I'm not your therapist. I'm a bartender, and I'm cutting you off."

"I'm not drunk."

"I don't care. Go home. I'm tired of watching you sulk."

He sat up and stared at her. "You're kicking me out?"

"Well, I'd like you to pay for your beer first." She folded her arms across her chest and stared right back at him.

What the hell? He reached into his pocket, pulled out his wallet, and threw a ten-dollar bill down on the bar.

"Do you need change?"

"Keep it." He shoved his wallet into his pocket so hard he heard fabric tear. What the fuck ever.

"Good night." Kim crossed her arms over her chest and gave the door a pointed glare.

He studied her for a long moment. Dark circles under her eyes, mouth flattened into a thin line. She was exhausted. And dead serious.

"Fine. Good night."

"If you want to see your nephew this weekend—"

He turned and walked away before she could finish the sentence, shoving through the heavy door to the bar and out into the cold, windy parking lot. Dusk was falling over the beach, and the whole world was as gray as he felt.

A car door slammed nearby, and he flinched from the noise, then unlocked his truck and climbed inside.

He banged his hand down on the steering wheel, scowling. Then did it again, and his hand hurt, but he didn't care. The third time, he hit the horn and the blast startled him. *Damn it.*

A soft knock sounded to his left. Kim. Fuck. She was crying. He rolled down the window.

"I'm sorry." She sniffled and reached through the window, placing her hands on the sides of his face. "I love you."

"Why?"

"Because you're my brother. And because you're wonderful. And I don't know what crawled up your ass and died, but you're scaring the shit out of me."

"Do you know how things ended with Ryan?"

She took a step back and shook her head, then came back to the window. "No. That was months ago. He went back to LA, and I thought you seemed okay."

He blew out an angry breath. "I am *not* okay."

"Hold on, I'm coming in."

She walked around the truck and climbed in the passenger side as he rolled the window back up.

"What about the bar?"

"There are three people in there; Candace can handle it. Tell me what happened with Ryan."

"He invited me to visit him in LA, and I called him a child."

She stared at him. "Why would you do that?"

"Because I'm an asshole and I hate myself. I don't *know*. I have no idea why I said it. I certainly don't think he's a child. We were fighting, but— I knew what Hollywood meant to him and I made it all or nothing."

She sighed and leaned her head on his shoulder. "You said it because you're terrified and ashamed of being terrified."

He scowled, but tipped his head to the side so it rested on hers. "Maybe."

"Are you going to let Vincent ruin everything, forever?"

"Maybe."

"Do you love Ryan?"

He didn't answer at first because the word had always seemed like such a nice word. Love was a nice thing for nice people. Ryan had *loved* him and it had been beautiful, but it *had* to end because he didn't deserve—

"Love isn't very nice, is it?"

She sat up straight and grasped his chin in her palm, turning him to face her. "Love is wonderful and terrible, and no, it isn't very nice. But you get to choose whether it's the best part of your life or the worst."

"Are you sure you're not a therapist?" He smiled sadly.

"I wish I got paid like one. What are you going to do?"

"He's gotten on with his life. I missed my shot, and now . . . I don't know. I figure out how to get on with mine."

Except he wasn't. He was wallowing in misery like it was his job.

"Maybe you should call. Text him. I don't know, I'm pulling this out of my ass here, but have you thought about apologizing?"

"Apologizing?"

"You know, that thing you do when you hurt someone."

"I know what an apology is."

She practically growled. "So you realize you owe him one?"

"Why would he want to hear from me?"

"Okay, I'm going back inside. We almost got somewhere for a minute there. Almost. Next time you're in a shitty mood, call Doc Wharton."

The door slammed behind her, and even though he *knew* she was right, *knew* he should see Doc Wharton, he let the fury boil over instead.

He drove home, kicked the door of his truck closed, and marched inside. Ferdy whined and tilted his head as Trey dumped food in the stainless steel dog dish and dropped it unceremoniously on the floor.

Even his damn dog was rebuking him.

Was this the life he wanted?

He turned on the TV and started flipping through the channels looking for a game—any game—to distract him, until a familiar sight stopped him cold.

Ryan.

The paramedic's uniform clung to his chest and shoulders, and in that particular scene—where he was braced over a patient, giving CPR—*oh holy night, his ass.* Trey's mouth went dry.

He wanted *that*. Not the ambulance ride with a paramedic straddling him—no, thank you, once in a lifetime was enough. But Ryan's attention, Ryan's body, Ryan's hair—what the fuck had he done to his head? The military-short buzz cut was hot—but there was nothing left to grab, and that realization was a bitter pang in Trey's chest. Ryan had changed—of course actors were chameleons—but Trey hadn't been there to witness it. To share in it. To rub the freshly shaved buzz for luck.

He'd missed it. And it was his fault.

Chapter Twenty-Five

A Mohawked black woman at the reception desk at the Adams Casting Agency gave Ryan a once-over above the tops of her clear-rimmed Warby Parkers and held up her finger. She radiated a cool, edgy elegance in her ice-blue suit and huge hoop earrings, and was speaking what sounded like Japanese into her cell phone. When she hung up, she asked, "Audition?"

He threw on as much charm as he could manage and grinned. "Am I that obvious?"

"You're not carrying donuts—not that anyone in LA *eats* donuts—so you can't be a salesman." She smirked. "You're a little old for the role, aren't you? I'm Chihiro Adams—please forgive our mess, we just moved into this space. Diane, my receptionist, landed a walk-on role on a sitcom at the last minute, and I keep accidentally calling my mother instead of answering the phone."

"Ryan—Bryan Hart."

"Bryan Hart— Oh." She tapped at the screen of a tablet perched on the desk. "You're not reading today."

"What?" Oh for fuck's sake, had they cast the role already and forgotten to call Mike?

"We're auditioning for the male lead—the seventeen-year-old male lead."

"I see. Okay."

Well, damn. He really was too old to play a teenager on television. It appeared he'd be taking that film role after all. Pulling his phone from his pocket, he fired off a quick text to Mike.

They're auditioning a different role today. Office a shambles, they just moved in.

Mike's reply came almost instantly. *I spoke to the show runner yesterday. Check again.*

"Ms. Adams? You might want to check your appointment list, because I was here to read for the teacher role—"

She held up a finger, her eyes widening as she read something on the screen of her tablet. "Mr. Hart, can you just—can you just sit for a minute?"

Disappearing around a corner with her cell phone pressed to her ear, she looked as panicked and stressed out as he felt. When she reappeared, loose-limbed and smiling, his stomach dropped. She was obviously vindicated, and he'd fucked up. Or his agent had. What did it matter? He started tapping out another text. *I'm in for Tex*

"Mr. Hart?"

The concern in Ms. Adams's voice brought his chin jerking up.

"Hi, I'm sorry for interrupting you, and again, I apologize for the mix-up. Mr. Brady is sending someone down for you."

Ryan's stomach resurfaced and his heart fluttered. He shoved his phone back in his pocket without sending the message. "West? West Brady?"

"Yes, sir. Mr. Brady is the show runner, and he'll be directing the pilot we're casting. I'm so sorry, I didn't realize you had a direct appointment with him."

"I didn't either—my agent didn't mention I was auditioning for West—Mr. Brady's—show. He and I know each other—" *don't say biblically, you idiot* "—socially."

She smiled warmly. "It may be a few minutes before his assistant makes it down here. Can I get you anything? A bottle of water? Coffee?"

"No, thank you."

He hadn't seen West since he and Ali had eloped shortly after the summer-stock season had begun. He'd seen Ali a handful of times, but only once since tiny Bea Brady had made a rushed, slightly early arrival at the end of October.

"Bryan?" A pale, freckled man in a gray suit with a bright-pink bow tie approached, walking with a quick, assured step. When he reached Ryan, he extended a hand. "I'm Calvin Reynolds, West Brady's PA."

Ryan blinked—taken aback by the man's deep low-country accent, then shook the proffered hand. "Um, hi. What happened to . . . Camryn?" He hoped he'd gotten her name right.

"Camryn has taken a job with Warner Bros. We're all very happy for her," he said in a flat tone.

"I see."

"If you'll follow me, Mr. Brady and his co-exec are waiting for you."

Ryan followed Calvin to the elevator, and they rode in awkward silence to the thirtieth floor. West. Why the hell hadn't Ryan asked for more details on this project? Was he so wrapped up in his own self-loathing he'd let himself be blindsided by a casting call from a dude he knew . . . *socially*?

As they stepped off the elevator, Calvin gave him a gentle smile. "You were my favorite in *Gravity Wells*. I know it's not appropriate to fanboy at work. But sometimes I can't help myself."

Ryan blushed. "Thanks. That's nice to hear. Too bad it got canceled, eh?"

"Oh, I don't know. You wouldn't be here if it hadn't been, and that would be a shame." Calvin opened a door on his right and held it for Ryan, who took a deep breath and walked inside to meet his fate.

West sat at the end of a long conference table, and next to him, positively radiant—and positively delighted with herself—was Ali.

Calvin quietly shut the door behind Ryan. Ali leaped to her feet, ran over, and hugged him tightly. "Are you surprised? I wanted you to be surprised. Chihiro accidentally gave it away downstairs, but damn, the expression on your face when you walked in here and saw me was priceless."

"Are you fucking kidding me? I was shitting myself in the elevator. You're the co-exec? That's—that's really super awesome."

"Hi, Ryan." West stood and came over to embrace him. "It's good to see you, buddy."

"It's good to see you too. Um, congratulations, you know, about the elopement and the baby and stuff."

West's broad grin warmed his whole face. "Thanks, Ry. Why don't you have a seat and we'll go over our vision for this role. If you're interested, we'd like some of the kids auditioning for the teenage lead to read with you this afternoon."

"Is this—is this an offer? Because—"

"We'll negotiate through Mike. But you're our first choice."

Wow. This afternoon was giving Ryan whiplash.

"Before we get started, I want to make it clear that if the series is picked up, the entire first season will be shot on location in North Carolina. Is that going to be a problem for you?"

Ryan's heart sank. At the beginning of the summer, he'd have given his right nut to have a movie offer. At the end of the summer, he'd have given his left nut to have a job offer allowing him to stay in North Carolina.

If he said yes, would Trey even want to see him? In hindsight, Ryan wished he'd been more patient with Trey that last morning in Banker's Shoals—but like everything else in his life, he'd rushed in feelings-first and made a mess. He wouldn't blame Trey if he didn't want to reconcile—but could Ryan bear to be so close to Trey and not *with* him?

"How soon do you need my decision?"

Walking up the steps to Trey's house, Ryan felt a flutter of nerves in his belly and a roil of nausea. Something was off, and he couldn't pinpoint what until he rang the bell and . . . nothing. No barking. Nothing. Maybe they were out for a walk?

He peered through the window in the door, but he couldn't see anything. He crossed back over to his brand-new car and searched inside for paper to write a note on. All he had was a Starbucks napkin. It would have to do.

Trey—I'm in town, staying at West's place for the weekend. Call me? I need to see you.

Love,

Ryan

He walked back up the steps, opened the screen and tucked the note between the doorframe and the doorknob. Taking a deep breath, he let the screen door close and started toward his car, disappointment bitter on his tongue.

Well, what the fuck had he expected? That he could just show up, knock on the door, and be welcomed with open arms like this was some Meg Ryan and Tom Hanks movie? As he sat there, berating himself for his stupidity, a truck rumbled into the driveway next to him. He lifted his head. Stared.

Trey.

Trey stared back, then slowly got out of his truck, walked around Ryan's car, and opened the driver's-side door.

"What are you doing here?"

"I needed to see you. I needed—" Ryan stood up. "God, you look so fucking good."

Trey smiled, but it didn't reach his eyes. "Let's go inside. We need to talk."

An icy chill slid down Ryan's spine. "You've met someone else, haven't you?"

"Just come inside, Ryan."

"Where's Ferdy?"

"He's at Kim and Danny's place."

"Oh."

Trey opened the screen door and the napkin fluttered to the ground. Raising an eyebrow at Ryan, he picked it up and read it, then smiled and tucked it into his back pocket.

Ryan stared at it for a moment while Trey unlocked the front door. Could the ground please open up and swallow him right here, right now?

When the door swung open though, his embarrassment was forgotten. "Holy shit, dude, have you been robbed?"

The place was a mess. But an . . . empty . . . mess. No sign of Trey's impeccable housecleaning. And . . . shit. Those were moving boxes stacked in the corner.

"I haven't been robbed."

"You're moving?" Ryan's heart sank.

"Not exactly. Just putting some stuff in storage because I'm going out of town and don't know how long I'll be gone. Didn't want to worry about possible damage if there's a flood."

The unfairness of it all stung so badly, Ryan wanted to punch something. "I couldn't drag you from this island kicking and screaming before, but now you're going traveling?"

Trey unlocked his phone, swiped the screen a few times, and handed it to Ryan. It took a few seconds for the information on the screen to register. When it did, his breath caught.

"You bought a one-way ticket to LAX?"

"Yeah."

"You trying to make it in Hollywood?" Okay, so, those were fucking tears in his eyes and he didn't fucking care because Trey had bought a one-way ticket to Hollywood, and Ryan was pretty sure he was the only person Trey knew in Hollywood.

"I messed up. I've made a lot of mistakes in my life. Marrying Vincent. Not leaving him sooner. Moving here with him. But I think maybe the biggest mistake I've ever made was making you believe I didn't care what you wanted. Making you feel like you didn't matter. You matter so much. And I wanted to be with you so badly. You were right, Ryan. I'm sorry. I love you. I was going to go to LA and try to win you back. I don't even know how. But I had to start with an apology. I owed you that. I— Wait. What the hell are you doing here?"

Ryan swallowed and reached for Trey. "I'm spoiling your grand gesture, you big jerk. I fucking love you. I took a TV job in North Carolina, because once you asked me to stay. I hoped you'd still want me."

Trey grabbed him, pulled him into a rough embrace, then kissed him, hard and biting, and they both started laughing into the kiss. Yeah, Trey wanted him.

"Please promise that you won't ever stop laughing when I kiss you. I'm so sorry."

"Apology accepted, but Trey—I'm sorry too. I know you've been through hell, and it was wrong of me to expect you to just get over it and change your whole life for me."

Trey shuddered. "I need to tell you something."

Ryan stepped away and met Trey's worried gaze. "What's up?"

"I'm still dealing with a lot of fallout from Vincent. I'm having to learn how to live with being scared and angry out of the blue and finding constructive ways to manage those emotions." He made a face. "Ugh, I sound like my shrink. I'm working on it, is the thing."

"Okay." Ryan nodded. "I'm glad. Is there anything I can do?"

"Maybe you can come to a therapy session with me and talk to Doc Wharton about that?"

"Whatever you need."

"You. I need you. I never got a chance to tell you how much I love you."

Ryan gasped as Trey's lips, then teeth found that sweet spot behind his ear. "Then show me."

Epilogue

"**C**ut!"

Ryan turned away from the camera and drew in a deep, shaky breath. He'd just filmed the most intense scene of his life, and the physical and emotional strain had been tearing at him all day. They'd ended the season on a dramatic cliff-hanger, only revealed to the cast that week, and his heart was beating fast.

"That's a wrap on season one. Thank you for your hard work, everyone." West moved around the set, shaking hands as the cast, crew, and the few audience members allowed on set applauded the season finale. When he got to Ryan, he pulled him into a hug.

"Bravo, you excellent fucker. That was some fine television we just made."

"*Goddamn*, you and Ali make a great writing team. If you don't get an Emmy for this shit, society is broken."

Ali wrapped her arms around his waist from behind and whispered her congratulations in his ear. As he looked over his shoulder and saw the small audience who had collected to watch the filming, he couldn't help but be proud of what West and Ali and their ragtag cast of character actors and newcomers had accomplished.

A teenage schoolhouse drama that was as riveting for adults as it was for teens? That didn't belittle them or talk down to them, but respected who they were and the difficulties in their lives? That featured a diverse cast of characters across multiple ethnicities, and sexual and gender identities? Yeah, he was damned proud of that.

"Where's Trey?"

"He and Kim took Bea and Jamie outside when we came back from the break. They didn't want the babies crying on set."

Ryan smiled. Trey's nephew and Bea had been born on the same day on opposite coasts, and Ali and Kim had grown close over the last few months.

Ryan made his way out of Banker's Shoals High School, where they'd filmed many of the schoolhouse scenes, and onto the football field, where Kim was sprawled on a blanket with Jamie, and Trey had a crying Bea in a sling. His attempts to woo her with a bottle were met with a pout and a shove against his chest. He kept trying though, and it made Ryan smile.

"Hey, you," he called.

Trey glanced up and waved. "Are you guys done in there?"

"Yup."

"Thank god. I think this kid wants boob, and I can't help her."

As he walked past, he stopped to kiss Ryan, thoroughly and deeply, and laughter bubbled up between them.

"I'll wait."

Trey came back a few minutes later, a wide smile on his beautiful face and the baby still snuggled to his chest. "She and Calvin are talking, but she said she'd be out in a minute. So, America's favorite teacher. How was class?"

Who would have thought taking a role as a high school teacher—one barely older than the students he taught—would turn out to be the most riveting role of his career? "School's out for summer."

"So what are you going to do now?"

"Mason offered to let me play Oberon."

"Summer stock again?"

"Yeah. Live theater—there's nothing like it."

They walked hand in hand back toward the set, stopping for a familiar face.

"Ryan, Trey!"

"Annsley!" Ryan hugged her tightly. The last time he'd seen her, she'd been covered in fake blood.

"Thank you for recommending me." She pulled out of the hug and put a hand on his shoulder. "This is an awesome credit for my résumé."

"I'm sorry it was just for three episodes." He grimaced. "I *told* Ali not to kill off the lesbian."

Annsley stuck her tongue out. "Believe me, I wish I hadn't had to play that scene. Shit, here she comes."

"Talking trash?" Ali winked at Ryan as she scooped Bea out of Trey's sling. "Hiya, Bea-bea. How's Mommy's girl?"

"You don't get to kill the lesbian and not have queer folk talk trash." Ryan crossed his arms over his chest.

"Annsley, call your agent." Ali, by some magic known only to nursing mothers, managed to get Bea latched on to her breast while digging the fingernails of one hand into Ryan's arm. "And you, darling, should probably read next season's script before you go posting your next AMA on Reddit."

"We've been renewed?"

"Yes, fucker." West came up alongside Ali. "We've been renewed." He grinned down at his wife and baby, face going all soft. "For two more seasons."

"I'm going to go call my agent." Annsley gave Ryan's hand a quick squeeze. "I suppose stabbings aren't always fatal?"

Next to Ryan, Trey flinched.

"Let's go," Ryan whispered, and Trey nodded.

"It's been a pleasure, Ali, West, Annsley. I'll see y'all later."

Trey echoed Ryan's sentiment in fewer words and a curt wave.

As they crossed the parking lot to the security perimeter, Trey slid his big, warm hand into Ryan's.

"All of this—and I do mean all of it—is okay with me."

"I'm sorry about what Ann said. She didn't know."

"Ryan . . ." Trey turned Ryan around so his back was pressed to Trey's chest and pointed out at the shoreline, just visible behind the school. "I used to be jealous of the sand. It got swept out and away while I was stuck here like a lighthouse with the waves beating against me. You hear me?"

Ryan turned around and touched Trey's lips. "You brought me home safely."

"Caro warned me that you'd never call Banker's Shoals home."

"I think it's time I learned to eat crow."

"Yeah?"

"As long as you're here, Banker's Shoals is definitely home."

Dear Reader,

Thank you for reading Vanessa North's *Summer Stock*!

We know your time is precious and you have many, many entertainment options, so it means a lot that you've chosen to spend your time reading. We really hope you enjoyed it.

We'd be honored if you'd consider posting a review—good or bad—on sites like **Amazon, Barnes & Noble, Kobo, Goodreads, Twitter, Facebook, Tumblr,** and your blog or website. We'd also be honored if you told your friends and family about this book. Word of mouth is a book's lifeblood!

For more information on upcoming releases, author interviews, blog tours, contests, giveaways, and more, please sign up for our weekly, spam-free newsletter and visit us around the web:

Newsletter: tinyurl.com/RiptideSignup
Twitter: twitter.com/RiptideBooks
Facebook: facebook.com/RiptidePublishing
Goodreads: tinyurl.com/RiptideOnGoodreads
Tumblr: riptidepublishing.tumblr.com

Thank you so much for Reading the Rainbow!

RiptidePublishing.com

Acknowledgments

Thanks to my wonderful editor, Caz, and to the rest of the Riptide team for putting their all into every book we create together. Your relentless pursuit of excellence makes me a better writer, and I'm grateful every day.

The two plays performed by Shakespeare by the Sea are William Shakespeare's *Julius Caesar* and *Much Ado About Nothing*. While there are many sources online for these public domain works, I referred frequently to shakespeare.mit.edu during my research.

Also by
Vanessa North

Blueberry Boys
Hostile Beauty
The Dark Collector
High and Tight
The Lonely Drop

Lake Lovelace Universe
Double Up
Rough Road
Roller Girl

How We Began: A Song for Sweater-boy
Lucky's Charms: Seamus
Love in the Cards: Two of Wands

About
The Author

Vanessa North is a writer of queer romance, a mother to twin boys, and a knitter of strange and wonderful things. She is the author of the Lambda Literary Award finalist *Blueberry Boys* and the Lake Lovelace series from Riptide Publishing. She once dedicated a book to Twitter, because she's classy like that. Follow her there and everywhere to be treated to photos of her very, very large dog.

Website: vanessanorth.com
Twitter: twitter.com/byvanessanorth
Instagram: instagram.com/vanessanorth
Facebook Group: facebook.com/groups/1188112571212585
Newsletter Signup: vanessanorth.com/newsletter-signup